Passage of the Fae

by Matthew E. Nordin

enjoy & keep imagining!

Shadows of Eleanor

book four

Matthew Nordin

This is a work of fiction. All of the characters, organizations, and events portrayed in his novel are either products of the author's imagination or are used fictitiously.

Cover art by BetiBup33 Design Studio
https://betibup33.com

Passage of the Fae / Shadows of Eleanor, book 4
ISBN: 978-1-7355573-3-5

For my fae who caught this poet's heart.

A fantastical retelling of how we met.

Passage of the Fae

Across the terrors of the sea,

We will journey 'til we are free.

Keep on rowing through darkened tide.

We will not let our courage hide.

Though monsters press upon our keel,

We will not become death's next meal.

And if others threaten our trip,

We will rely upon our ship,

For they should fear our mighty name.

The tide can bring us to great fame.

With hearts more fierce than any shark,

The tide inhales up from the dark.

Yet if we hit that fateful squall,

The tide must rise and also fall.

And like the waves upon the stone,

The tide will wash away our bone.

- A song composed by Aldrnari,

whose pages sunk to a watery abyss.

1

A loud creak from the ropes on the loosened sail caused Aldrnari to survey the sky. The Stormeye's black flag swayed like the rushing of its crew across the weathered planks. Great billows of violent clouds collected in front of them, blocking the path they needed to reach the port. The storm hadn't moved in days.

"All hands, swift to scurry," a deep voice shouted from the captain's cabin.

The monstrous figure hastening his steps to the wheel left Aldrnari with a wary gaze. For years he had traveled with little stop at land. Whenever they did land, his captain, Crowell, kept the cabin boy locked in a room. The ship needed to break through the thunderous rain so he could make his escape.

"Are we going to press onward?" Aldrnari asked as he moved out of the captain's way.

Crowell gave him a nod of acknowledgment.

"This storm hasn't diminished," the pirate at the wheel narrowed her eyes at their destination. "It's completely impassable."

The female helmsman who piloted the Stormeye stood taller than any of the lesser sailors. Her lanky frame swayed listlessly with the increasing wind. Yet her stature barely reached Crowell's shoulders as he loomed over her.

Another crack from the rigging warned the crew of their doom if they attempted to force their way through the immovable storm.

"I've no doubt you would survive it," she continued. "But I'm not sure how the rest of us may fare."

Crowell took off his hat and stared into the dark wall of rain ahead.

"You are correct, Brittany," he said and flashed his jagged teeth. "This storm hasn't changed since we arrived. Double back at once."

Aldrnari wanted to groan at Brittany's influence over Crowell but decided not to show any displeasure. A dark rage would often consume the captain, sending anyone who disagreed to a watery tomb. This made his desire to leave stronger and more hopeless.

"I think we could sail around it," Aldrnari said and pulled out his maps.

A hush fell across the rest of the crew as they stepped back. No breath condensed in the frosty air.

Crowell's hulking frame moved toward the young cabin boy. "How long would it take to reroute our approach?"

"If it's not moving, we should be able to find a safe passage around the eastern edge of it." Aldrnari trembled while he focused on keeping his voice steady. They had never been so close to Northeal, and it would be the perfect place to flee. "I don't have a good answer for you. It may take some time."

"These storms should not waste our time any longer." A tendon in Crowell's neck flared as he clenched his fists. "We will return to open water. Ready the sails."

The captain retreated to his cabin faster than he emerged. The entire hull of the ship shook when he slammed the door, darkening the mood of his crew.

Aldrnari thought about convincing Brittany to continue around the surge, but she would not go against the captain's orders.

"Can you slow our departure?" Aldrnari asked her. "I want to recheck my maps. It's possible we can gain entry to the port without much delay."

"You heard Crowell," Brittany said without moving. "He doesn't want to waste any more time here."

"I understand," Aldrnari sighed. "I'm going to check my maps to be sure. I'll be below deck."

Brittany turned to him and studied his face. She always had a way of knowing what he thought before he told her. He hoped she couldn't figure out his true intentions and blinked rapidly, looking to the deck. If he made it to a longboat in time, no one would notice.

Being shorter than the rest of the crew gave him an advantage to sneak around the lower deck. His crop of black hair contrasted with the deep blue of his eyes and tanned skin. Some said he daydreamed too much, and he had to admit it was mainly due to his wanderlust. He frequently escaped in his mind to different places and wrote them into poetry.

Aldrnari tucked his overstuffed book of poetry into a bag with some maps and crept toward the longboats. Getting around the storm would be easier in a smaller vessel. Not being seen while the crew was on high alert would test his abilities.

"You should work on your stealth," Brittany said as Aldrnari knocked over the oars lined up on the wall.

He hung his head, trying to catch his breath. "These weren't fastened properly, and I wanted to make sure they were secure if Crowell changes his mind about the storm."

"I see." Brittany picked one up and tapped the end in her other hand. "There's no other reason you'd be down here, is there?"

Aldrnari looked around and noticed they were alone. He wanted to tell her of his grand plan to escape. It had taken up most of his thoughts while they waited at the storm front.

Initially, he hoped to find a way around it with the Stormeye. After a few well-placed distractions, he would jump off and swim under the docks. His breathing exercises helped him focus and would be useful in keeping him submerged.

His secondary strategy was less developed, and Brittany seemed to be picking up on his lack of planning.

"If I linger from the wheel for too long, the others may notice," she said. "You, however, are often missed by our captain alone."

Aldrnari couldn't tell if she was being sincere or cruel. "You wouldn't miss me if I disappeared?" He tried to be charming, but Brittany always saw him as a child.

"Where would we be without our little poet?" she scoffed. "Honestly, we took you—I mean, we found you way too young. You wouldn't survive on your own."

"There's not much I contribute here. Crowell never uses my maps except to check against his own." Aldrnari sat on one of the supply crates. "I've never understood why you two are so protective of me. There's more to the world than endless waves."

She leaned against the wall and looked toward the ceiling. "You get this way whenever we get close to a port. I'm surprised Crowell didn't lock you up yet. He favors you the most, like a pet."

Aldrnari hopped off the crate and wanted to defend himself against her comment, but she was right. Crowell and the others treated him more like a creature to be trained than a human with thoughts and dreams.

"I suppose pets must eventually find their way back to the wild," Brittany said. "If you want to go unnoticed, you should loosen that one." She pointed to the smallest vessel covered in discarded sails. "Not many know it's there."

She placed a finger to her lips and turned swiftly to the stairs leading back to the deck.

The raft resembled a sleek canoe with room for one and limited supplies. The way its previous occupant had stuffed it among the dusty crates assured Aldrnari that Brittany told the truth—no one would miss it.

He moved more cautiously to clear it free of the debris than he did around the oars.

A spark of hope bolstered his confidence, and he edged the front of the boat out one of the portholes. It would be able to slip out with little effort as long as he didn't try jumping out with it or overloading the seats.

"I'm sure they won't miss these," he said and rummaged through the crates for canned food.

Footfalls above alerted him of the crew's readiness to depart. The Stormeye was fleeing the storm.

After he secured his bag and supplies into the tiny vessel, he fastened a rope around its frame. The wood knocked against the larger ship's hull while he lowered it through the opening. His fingers turned white as he gripped the tether. A leap of faith into the open water was all he had left to do.

Images of his life on the Stormeye flashed through Aldrnari's mind. A few good memories and the growing fear in his gut urged him to stay, but he'd never get a chance like this again. He closed his eyes and stepped forward.

2

Aldrnari's body escaped into the open air before it plummeted to the waves. With a gasp of breath, he hit the surface and disappeared from those who held him captive.

The cold sea bit against his limbs while he slowly swam up with the rope's help. He'd likely be spotted if he moved too quickly, but at the same time, he could drift too close to the storm. His mind numbed with the rest of his body while he held his breath. The dropping temperature and adrenaline wanting to burst through his chest didn't help.

He reached the top of the rope and lifted his head from the water, enough to let the air fill his lungs. With a final tug, he managed to pull himself onto the bench of his drifting vessel. The salt stung his eyes, but he could see the Stormeye departing in the opposite direction from him.

"I need to keep moving," he urged himself as the looming clouds darkened around him.

The waves would be too fierce to row against if he delayed. He steadied his gaze on the expanse he needed to cross and hooked the oars into their notches.

It took longer than he planned to clear himself from the storm and get positioned in the right current.

"There should be more ships out here," he said and reached for his map.

To his surprise, his hand hit water before the bag. The shock made him aware of how much of the sea he'd taken on since his departure.

One of the larger tins of food had already opened, spoiling the contents inside. Aldrnari quickly emptied the rest of it over the side and used it to bail out the growing pool inside his boat. It helped a little, but water continued to leak between the cracks of the boards.

He got enough out to grab his bag and place it on his lap. Water dripped down his legs while his heart sank. A glance inside was enough to see the ink smeared across the papers. All of his drawings, poems, and musings were banished to the salty sea.

The bag fell to his side, and he let it slip back down. Tears wanted to overtake his eyes, but he took in a deep breath to still the sadness. His words may be lost from the page, but they remained in his mind . . . most of them.

Survival overcame any further thoughts of how he could recover his lost writings as the boat sprouted another leak.

"Please give me a break," Aldrnari cried out.

He grabbed another can and held it against the hole. It stopped the flow, but he could not keep it there and continue rowing. Remembering when he watched the crew address a similar issue, he used his other supplies to create a wedge against the can.

Unfortunately, Aldrnari had nothing to mend it permanently. Water continued to ooze in as he increased his pace. He found the leather covers of his books worked as better seals for the many holes that sprang between the shoddy boards.

The more he rowed, the more his energy dwindled. Switching between bailing out water and continuing forward became exhausting. Brittany likely knew the boat was in such bad condition. He should have learned not to trust her. She envied the favoritism shown to him by their captain, who was possibly on the hunt for him already.

Crowell had given countless warnings about the consequences of fleeing from the Stormeye. No port would be safe from the captain's reach. And one of the largest ones became further away as more water burst into Aldrnari's vessel.

"This is useless," he said in defeat and took off his boots.

He tied them around his belt, removing his outer vest to prepare for the inevitable swim. The gentle rocking helped him relax and focus on his breathing. He paddled steadily toward the dock, hoping his mental map of the currents was correct.

The sun sunk into the ocean's horizon, as did his tiny vessel. At least he would have the cover of night when he arrived—if his muscles continued to move through the pain burning through every part of him.

Aldrnari struggled to stand, let alone walk, when the tide finally carried him close enough to shore. The main port of Northeal remained a short distance from where he climbed the broken boulders along the coast. Thankfully, he had enough sense to put his boots back on before traversing the slippery and dangerous surface. A few cuts across his pants reminded him to take his time. The worst was behind him, he hoped.

Avoiding the crowded areas of Northeal had been part of his plan, but the current floated him a little farther than he wanted. Physically, his body felt like it had given up with the rest of his belongings, sinking with the tattered boat. Mentally, he knew he had to keep moving.

A lingering scent from a bakery hit Aldrnari's nostrils when he reached the outskirts of town. Food consumed his thoughts and made him forget he was wandering through an alley, likely an unsavory one.

The two-story buildings were dark, not producing a sound of who or what lived inside. Rumbles from the storm in the distance and Aldrnari's shambling footsteps provided a break in the stillness of the night.

Behind a box with half of its sides missing, he thought he saw something move.

"Is someone there?" he whispered.

A muddy canvas flapped against the wall as he crept closer.

He breathed a sigh of relief. There wasn't a big enough space for anyone to hide, but something else caused the hair on the back of his neck to prick up.

A voice muttered behind him.

Aldrnari spun around with his hands up to defend himself.

The man standing before him repeated the indistinguishable phrase and held out an open palm. His ragged clothes and wild hair suggested the man had been through much worse than a shipwreck. Yet a kindness in his eyes eased his features.

"I wish I could help you," Aldrnari said and relaxed his arms back to his side. "I've lost everything too."

The stranger pointed to the pouch on Aldrnari's belt and mumbled again at him.

"I'm sorry." Aldrnari reached into the empty bag. "I don't—"

He trailed off as his fingers came across a metal disk, a coin. Its polished silver sparkled like new in the moonlight when he pulled it out to examine it closer.

A castle with a family crest marked one side, while the other had numbers and symbols he'd never encountered. It had to be rare and costly.

He looked at the beggar and once more at the coin. Given all of the items he'd taken from others in the past, his fingers clutched the coin tightly before he was able to stretch out his arm. Although momentary greed lingered in the back of his mind, the man needed it more than him.

"I'm not sure what this is worth." He dropped it into the beggar's hand. "I hope it brings you better luck in life."

The whiteness of the man's teeth flashed inside his broad smile. It caused Aldrnari to smile too.

"Before you go," Aldrnari continued. "Can you tell me of a place to stay for the night?"

The man nodded and rambled on in his foreign tongue. Aldrnari pretended to follow his explanation, but his inability to understand must have shown.

Without another word, the beggar pointed into the distance and turned him to face the direction.

Lightning flashed across the sky, illuminating a column of smoke rising from the chimney of a large tavern.

"Do I need to go there?" Aldrnari turned to ask the man, but he was gone.

A clap of thunder was all that responded.

Another streak of lightning lit the alley, much closer than the last one. The boom shook Aldrnari. Tiny drops of water fell into his hair.

He sighed and hung his head. Without any more warning, clouds engulfed the moon. The rain became more intense as he walked to the building.

A small object hit his ear. Balls of ice bounced off the cobblestone road after they fell from the sky. Aldrnari covered his head with his hands and ducked under the awnings of the buildings near him. They continued to give some relief from the storm as he raced down the path to the tavern.

3

Weariness overcame Aldrnari's ability for caution as he swung open the door to the tavern. The smell of food and a warm fireplace renewed his spirits. His boots squished mud and water onto the wood floor.

"Come in, lad," a voice greeted him from across the great room. "Get that door closed before you make us all soggy and miserable."

Aldrnari shut the door and approached the man at the bar. He felt oddly drawn to him.

The stranger wore a tricorn hat full of feathers, signifying the captain of a large vessel. Lines in his brown skin created hard edges to his face, not much older than the poet who stared for too long at him. A green hue in his eyes held a celestial wonder behind them—like they were as old as the earth itself and created their own trails of light.

"No need to be glum." The man apparently noticed the change in Aldrnari's expression. "We are passing through ourselves. I recognized the disoriented look when you entered. Come orient yourself in the right direction of a drink. The first one's on me." He knocked on the bar to get the matron of the tavern's attention. "Don't be afraid. Everyone's a stranger until you know them better. Those who do know me better like to call me Varn."

Aldrnari gave a weary smile and nodded. He grabbed a nearby stool.

"Ah, we have a table," Varn said before he could relax. "Jodoc's there now."

He waved to another man sitting at one of the booths. A pile of books almost hid him from view.

Jodoc perked up and gave a hearty wave in response. His beard wrapped around his face, and he tucked it in front of his robe. Sticking out of his straight hair was a pair of elongated ears.

At first, Aldrnari thought them to be a fashion accessory, but then he remembered hearing tales about elves. Crowell only associated with humans, so it was his first time seeing one in person. He was bigger than expected. The elf's broad shoulders and full belly made him look like a giant if he were standing.

"You a reader, lad?" Varn asked, nudging Aldrnari's arm. "You don't seem to be much of a talker."

"Sorry." He realized he'd been staring at both of them. "Yes, I do read. And I'm a writer. They call me Aldrnari, and I didn't plan to make it this far."

"Well, you made it. Let's get you some ale to loosen your tongue."

Aldrnari laughed from Varn's quick wit.

"Go on and sit with Jodoc," he continued. "I'll get the drinks and join you soon. There are some other things I need to settle here."

"Thank you." Aldrnari wanted to ask the matron about a room for the night but found himself more inclined to join the elf at their booth.

"Have a seat, have a seat," Jodoc said and stood for Aldrnari to get in.

As Aldrnari suspected, the elf towered above him.

Varn returned to the table at the same time Aldrnari managed to sit down. The matron of the tavern followed close behind him, carrying two drinks.

"Your friend here paid for this one," she dropped the mug in front of Aldrnari. Less of the ale spilled out than he imagined it would. "If you're planning on sticking around for another, we'll need to discuss if you're staying for the night. It's a bit too treacherous out there to have you wandering on your own. Especially with more than one of my drinks."

Aldrnari looked down at the liquid in his mug. It would likely be the last one he had for a while.

"Do you have any lodging available for a few nights?"

"Aye, for the right price." The matron crossed her arms.

His lack of funds must have been apparent.

"I don't have any coins on me, but I'm always good for work." He held up his empty pouch and shook it. Something clamored inside. "Wait a minute."

He opened it quickly and found two of the strange coins he had given to the beggar in the alley.

"Will these do?" Aldrnari handed them to her with less hesitation, wondering at their origin.

"Another one of your kin, I presume," the matron said as she took the coins and nudged Varn. "These will pay for your meals while you're here as well."

She gave Aldrnari a crooked smile before turning back to the bar. He caught a few of her mutterings which indicated he could have stayed for months with that amount.

Aldrnari could hardly taste the bitter grog as he drank it without taking a breath. It quenched his thirst but made his eyes water.

"If you don't mind me asking, where did you get those coins?" Varn leaned over the table to meet Aldrnari's gaze.

He wanted to lie and tell the captain he had a stash of them back home, but the same spark of kindness from the beggar rested in the man.

"I'm not sure," he confessed. "I entered town with nothing, and the coins appeared in my bag."

"Do you think he got the bag from another immortal?" Jodoc asked Varn. "I thought you'd said there were none quite like it."

"Indeed I did." Varn sat back and moved his hand from the table. Underneath it appeared another one of the silver coins. "If I were to guess, I'd say this boy hasn't met an immortal until now. Am I right?"

Aldrnari's mouth remained open, but no words came out. Rumors told of a race that could live forever and isolated themselves on a sacred island. Any sailor who sought them out never returned. Surely the man before him could not be one. His tone was too welcoming.

"I didn't know immortals left their homeland," Aldrnari managed to say and turned to Jodoc. "I thought you were an elf."

Jodoc leaned back and laughed. "That I am, that I am." He took a deep breath and composed himself. "We rarely leave our kingdom either, unless called upon by an immortal, fae, or important human. It was hard to part with the woods." His expression turned somber.

"You'll return someday," Varn said and pushed the coin in front of Aldrnari. "I'm giving this to you, but do not use it for yourself. I'm guessing the two you gave for your stay were the only ones in your bag, correct?"

Aldrnari nodded.

"The magic of the coins does not work unless you give them away. So this one is yours. If you want to double it, give it to someone in need and keep one for yourself. Never give away both." Varn took off his hat and rested it in front of him. "Since I have told you this, I'd like to ask for some information in return."

Aldrnari pondered a while about anything he knew that would be important to an immortal. "Although my physical maps were lost, I have a great memory of routes and currents across the sea. I learned where the trolls like to attack and where to summon the strongest creatures of the deep."

"Interesting." Varn took a drink of his ale, nearly downing it in one gulp. "This knowledge may prove useful in the future." He patted his chest to keep from burping. "What I need to know is simple, where did you come across the silver coin?"

"There was a beggar outside asking for money, and it was suddenly there when I went to show him that I had nothing." Aldrnari wished he knew where the stranger went. "I swear my bag was empty."

"Did the beggar tell you his name? Did he perform any magic? Where did you see him?"

Aldrnari scooted back as he feared Varn might grab him by the collar to shake out his answers. "He was in an alley near the edge of town—west. I'm pretty sure. I couldn't understand what he was saying, so he might have given me his name. I don't know."

Varn stroked his raven goatee and appeared to be lost in thought.

"His eyes were similar to yours," Aldrnari continued. "Is that important?"

"That's the best information I've gotten since arriving here." Varn smiled and pulled out a standard gold coin. He flicked it across the table. "Use this to buy yourself another drink. Your information was better than mine."

Without another word, Varn grabbed his hat and fastened the buttons of his overcoat. He rushed to the door. A flash of lightning illuminated his silhouette before he disappeared into the night.

"What's his hurry?" Aldrnari asked Jodoc, who had been scribbling down some notes.

"It's the reason an elf and an immortal would be in Northeal," he said without looking up. "We've been searching for Varn's brother. He was one of the first immortals to leave the island in a very long time. Something was stirring in the world."

Jodoc set his pen down gently and folded a strap of leather around his journal. He made a gesture for the matron to bring more drinks before turning his attention to Aldrnari.

"His brother has been missing for many years," Jodoc said and took a slow sip from a fresh mug. "We came to this port because of the upcoming festival. Some said they saw the fae again near Caetheal, the village to the south. His brother was an emissary to them and kept close contact with us elves. Well, before the rupture."

"What was the rupture?" Aldrnari handed the gold coin to the matron.

"This night keeps blessing me," she said. "I hope your friend is okay in the storm. It's getting worse out there."

"He'll be fine," Jodoc said and waited for the hostess to return to the bar. "The hostility between the elves and humans was from something more sinister. Varn calls it a rupturing of the realms. A dark force upset the balance of the world. He said it's also why the fae stopped trading." He pulled out a map and pointed to a town bordering a great forest. "Their main place of business was down in Caetheal. Some said an immortal helped rebuild the town, and they're having festivals in the area. It supposedly lures some of the fae out of hiding."

"So Varn's brother will likely be there?"

"Exactly," Jodoc said.

The elf closed his eyes, and Aldrnari assumed he was saying a silent prayer. He used the opportunity to take a few sips of ale. The grog he experienced before was masked by a hot spice. The burning in his throat from the more potent alcohol caused him to choke.

"We did the same thing," Jodoc said with a big grin. "I was hoping you'd have a better reaction. I must admit I assumed a northerner like yourself would be able to hold it in a little longer."

"How do you know I'm from the north?" Aldrnari coughed.

"Well, you're definitely not from here, and you have a similar look to those in the northern lands. Varn and I searched there first for his brother."

"I grew up on a ship—taken when I was too young to remember and forbidden to talk about those places. It would make sense if my ancestors lived there. "

"Sorry to hear of the misfortune, but it seems your fate has changed." Jodoc gathered his books. "I should get back to my room. If you're inclined to see the festival tomorrow, be down here at first light. You don't want to miss breakfast."

"Thank you," Aldrnari said as Jodoc stood to leave. "I should find my room as well."

He let the sudden stillness of the table rest his mind a while longer. His muscles had finally warmed from the fireplace burning steadily on the other side of the room. The talk of fairies and traveling with Jodoc grew more appealing as he finished off another drink placed in front of him.

It might have been stronger than he assumed. After trying to recite some of his poetry to the matron, she showed him to his room. She shook her head and laughed while she left him to his thoughts.

Aldrnari kept enough of his wits to take off his boots before collapsing onto the bed. The ale and exhaustion overcame him as he cocooned himself in the blankets and dreamed of joining Varn's crew.

4

The morning sun caused Aldrnari to blink as he examined where he'd fallen asleep so soundly. It was a simple room with little more than a bed and chair. He looked down at the dirt imprint left on the bed from his hasty entrance.

Dust particles floated in a stream of light when he moved the covers. Their mesmerizing dance through the air held his attention until they caused him to sneeze, shaking his senses fully awake.

The sun had already traveled most of the morning sky, and he was late for breakfast.

Trying to navigate his way down the steps in a rush and with weary muscles proved challenging. If it weren't for the handrail, he likely would have tumbled down them.

After composing himself at the bottom, he surveyed the seemingly empty great room.

"There he is," a prominent voice called from one of the farthest tables, preceding a laugh from the other. "We thought it best to let you sleep a bit longer based on your recent endeavors. Didn't expect it to take half the morning."

"Wait, half the morning isn't gone already, is it?" Jodoc said as he moved the curtains near him.

Aldrnari rubbed his head and joined the two at their table.

"I let the barkeep know we would wait for you, so she didn't wake you early." Varn slid a plate full of eggs and sausage in front of Aldrnari. "If you waited any longer, you might have lost this meal. Jodoc suggested using a cold bucket of water, but I advised against it."

"Nothing like a good wash to get you up in the morning," Jodoc interjected with a jab from his elbow to the captain.

"Thank you for keeping me dry," Aldrnari said between bites. "I was wet enough from the storm. Speaking of, did you find the beggar I was telling you about?"

"Not yet." Varn sighed. "I'll find him when he wants me to. The way you described him makes me certain it was my brother.

He was always good at slipping from view. My guess is that he'll be at the festival. He likely started it."

"Please help me finish this so we can leave," Aldrnari said, trying to stuff in more of the lightly seasoned meat.

Its dry texture had to be washed down with extra amounts of water. He appreciated the large glass they had gotten for him.

"You don't have to twist my ears," Jodoc said and scooped some onto his plate.

"How far away is Caetheal? Will we miss most of it since I overslept?"

Varn looked at Jodoc, who had his mouth already full of eggs.

"We have time," the captain said. "The matron supplied us with a few spare tents since we've decided to end our stay. I assumed you're joining us."

Aldrnari nodded as he and Jodoc finished the rest of the plate.

"There are other supplies I'd like us to gather. Most of them are on the Tide's Requiem—my ship." Varn stood up and approached the matron at the bar.

"I'm glad you're coming with us," Jodoc said quickly. "I enjoy all kinds of literature and would like to hear some of your poetry."

"You would?" He finished the rest of his drink and tapped the side of the glass. "Unfortunately, my books were lost, but I do have many of them memorized."

"You can compose some new ones on our journey to the festival." Jodoc smiled and brushed off his robe. "Sadly, it's time for us to bid farewell to this cozy tavern."

He motioned to Varn, who grabbed the tents from the matron. The other two took their bags and bedrolls. Aldrnari hoped they didn't need too many supplies for the festival. He wasn't sure if he'd be able to make the journey with more weight —especially with how fast he ate.

"We'll need to grab our vestments for the festival," Varn said as he opened the door to let them out. "You could use some better ones yourself, lad. It looks like you just escaped from a dirty pirate ship."

Aldrnari smirked and tucked in his ratty clothes. A new wardrobe would be a welcome change.

"Thank you again for your hospitality," Jodoc said, tossing another coin to the matron. "We hope to find such fine establishments in our future travels. Light blessings to you."

The three ventured down the muddy streets toward the docks. The air smelled crisp from the rain. Aldrnari imagined how lucky they were the event did not happen during the storm. No doubt the weather would cause many complications to the foretold merriment.

To his surprise, the bustling harbor of Northeal was nearly empty. Some of the latecomers to port were being assisted by a few brutish men—one Aldrnari recognized.

"Look out," Aldrnari said and crouched behind a nearby crate. "There's someone up there from my former ship. He's probably looking for me. I can't go any further."

Varn knelt beside him. "Hold fast to your wits. You are one of us, which means you've no need to lose courage."

"I might have something to keep you hidden." Jodoc placed his bag on the ground. He rummaged through it and pulled out one of his cloaks. "This is a grand disguise, and none will be the wiser. I apologize for the plainness of it. It's drabber than my own."

The elf held it up to Aldrnari. The garment was meant for a taller person.

"I'm not sure it will fit well enough without me dragging it through the mud," Aldrnari said and looked around for a clothing shop.

"Trust me."

Jodoc threw the large fabric over Aldrnari's shoulders before he could protest more. The strings at the edges of the sleeves were tied into the cloak with Jodoc's quick movements. He did the same at the bottom seam and doubled the fabric near the waist before securing everything with a belt.

Although limited in his movement, the cloak resembled a robe and appeared to be a custom fit for Aldrnari.

"Thank you," he said and pulled the hood over his head.

The man he spied earlier seemed to be staring in their direction.

"I still shouldn't go anywhere near the docks," Aldrnari said, trying to keep his voice low. "I can get supplies in town. Is there a place we can meet up after you collect what you need?"

"Aye, there's a large market at the southern edge of town," Varn said and turned his back to the docks. "I'm sure we can find each other there. The main road through it continues down to Caetheal. Although it might be best for us to stick together."

Aldrnari backed into the shadows. "I don't want to get you two involved with my past."

"You'll need better garments for the festival," Jodoc said. "Mine will make you look too suspicious. They may not let you in."

"I left some hidden where I landed," he lied and looked back to the docks.

The man from before was gone. Maybe he'd imagined it. Or maybe his former crewmate was on the hunt for him.

"Be safe and make haste." Varn must have noticed the worry in Aldrnari's eyes. "We will do the same. Watch for the green cart. You'll likely not recognize us."

The captain winked and shoved Aldrnari into a hidden alleyway. He spun around and regained his footing before sprinting down the maze of passages. The open windows caused him to slow his pace and crouch down, ready for one of Crowell's crew to reach out and grab him. It was unnerving how dark each building remained in the late morning.

Aldrnari's heart raced as he stepped onto one of the merchant lanes. It was not only from running, but fear halted his ability to continue forward. Pulling the hood across his face, he closed his eyes. He couldn't let his past control his future.

"You there," someone called out from the row of tables. "You seem to require some beads, and I've got the perfect necklace to help on your pilgrimage."

Aldrnari wanted to ignore the vendor who had an overly groomed beard but noticed the person at the stall next to him selling all sorts of fine clothes. Vests, tunics, and expensive coats were hanging over the edges in an unorganized mess. A few had fallen to the ground.

"I am looking for new adornments," Aldrnari called back to the bead merchant.

He approached the table, making sure to step onto the discarded wares of the bearded man's neighbor. Although he nodded to act like he was interested in the man's well-intended sales pitches, he used the distraction to slip a few garments off the table. The extra fabric of Jodoc's robe provided him with room to stash his findings.

"Do you have anything that would work around my ankle?" he asked, crouching down. "The other town I visited had unique jewelry for one's foot."

"Ah, let's see what I might have back here for you." The merchant turned around, and Aldrnari quickly picked up as many clothes as he could carry. "This is more of a bracelet, but it may work for you," the man said, holding a small strand of pearls.

"Thank you for showing me all you have to offer and for your time," Aldrnari said, glancing south for an exit. "My friends and I will return this way after the festival. I wish you good fortune on your sales."

The man scoffed and twirled his beard. "The festival is full of overpriced charlatans. The cost to set up there is enough for an honest man to sell his home. When you're there, remember where to get the best-priced beads."

"I will." Aldrnari smiled politely at him and strolled to the edge of the merchant lane, being sure to appear like he was browsing as he passed other tables.

None of the others had their items so easily accessible as the clothier.

He soon found his way into an alley and loosened the garments he'd taken. Most of them were for everyday wear.

Setting everything onto a box in the lone street, he finished assembling a combination of the nicer ones. A tightly woven red shirt with dark stripes on the sleeves matched a black vest. They would give more flair to the plain pants he wore.

He decided to keep another white shirt and a simple red vest. It helped that each item looked to be fancy vestments of a sailor who took to port. He hoped his new companions wouldn't question where he acquired them.

Aldrnari left the remaining pile of clothes on the box. "Someone else could use these," he said to himself, trying to justify the number of items he'd stolen.

A tinge of guilt worked its way into his chest. It felt like people were watching him from every roof and window. While on the Stormeye, he had no shame taking another's belongings—mainly because they were pirated during their frequent raids.

The merchants in Northeal seemed to be working for an honest living. For the first time, he regretted the stolen clothes and vowed to make amends with the vendor when they returned from Caetheal.

Aldrnari took a deep breath and shook his head to clear away the new emotions. He had to focus on finding Varn and Jodoc, while also avoiding Crowell's crew. Fright from seeing one earlier spurred his feet to move swiftly as he made his way to the southern road out of town.

5

A breeze kicked up dust from the pilgrimage of travelers headed to Caetheal. Aldrnari wiped his eyes and lifted the collar of his shirt over his mouth. He tried to keep from coughing, but tiny particles filled his throat.

Jodoc sat beside him on the cart with narrowed eyes, unfazed by the wind blowing directly at them. He chuckled softly and handed Aldrnari a rag.

"Thank you," Aldrnari whispered with a rasp in his voice. He coughed intentionally to clear the debris in his lungs. "I've been wondering, how did you meet Varn?"

"Some are born to lead, others are born to follow," Jodoc said and shifted his position on the cart. He glanced ahead to Varn, who was walking with the horse pulling them. "I follow the light, which led me under his care. Each person must choose a master. Otherwise, they'll follow whatever sounds best at the time. There is a significant draw that brings others to desire the company of an immortal. I sense you have felt it as well." Jodoc paused for reflection. "The path each of us walks is full of darkness and doubt. Most seek the betterment of their own will. A few are sent to watch and protect others. You have to keep your eyes fixed on the light, and the darkness will not be able to overcome it. It will help guide us to find what we need. Be it fae or friends."

"I understand some of what you're saying," Aldrnari said and brushed the wrinkles from his vest. "It's hard to keep my hopes up when I have to watch my back. The ship I grew up on was not a kind place."

"Having an extra set of eyes helps when you're on the run." Jodoc gave him a wink. "Besides, Varn and I could fend off any of your former crew."

"I'm not sure how you would fare against Crowell. He's known as the fiercest pirate on the seas and challenges anyone who opposes him." Aldrnari looked behind him to make sure speaking the name hadn't somehow summoned his childhood captor. "I've never seen him fail in a fight."

"I'd enjoy matching swords with him then," Varn said, spinning around. "I've met no equal off the isle of immortals. Although, Jodoc came close." He pulled back his blood-red sleeve to reveal a small scar across his forearm. "Never using that defense again."

"It was a lucky counter," Jodoc said and laughed.

"Even still, you nearly caused a fatal wound."

Aldrnari scoffed. "How could you have a deadly blow? Aren't you supposed to be immortal?"

Varn stared at him like he didn't want to reveal his family secrets. "We are not unstoppable and eventually die. Our bodies just age differently from most races and heal rapidly. A direct strike to the heart or head would kill us stone dead." He put a finger to his lips. "But you never heard it from me. And the blade would have to be sharp enough to pierce our skin."

"Good thing you're wearing those garments," Jodoc added. "They keep anyone from thinking they have an advantage over an immortal. Deception can be a strong ally."

Varn nodded in agreement. His red shirt matched a few of the rare feathers in his cap and the embellishments on his boots. His sleeveless overcoat had silver floral designs with swords and dragons woven throughout.

Jodoc also wore a more formal robe. The dark brown was not faded by the sun, and it had bronze embellishments tapered along the edges. Long strings hung from the sleeves and around the waist to tie back for easier movement.

"I must confess something to you, lad," Varn said and hopped onto the cart. "We heard of you before you arrived in our company and had hoped to meet you."

Aldrnari was stunned by the statement. "How?"

"We were near the docks looking for my brother. A rowdy group of sailors was mentioning Crowell and how his ship had been spotted near Northeal. For their rough appearance, they sang great melodies. I managed to haggle one into divulging the writer's name. He informed me of a cabin boy they had on their ship—told me he could plot a course to anywhere and wrote in spite of their drudgery. He said the captain called you his northern poet." Varn turned to Jodoc. "We found the song quite catchy."

Jodoc smiled and sang:

Tie the anchor; hoist the sail. Straight through the waves we go.

Kiss your dear loved ones farewell. Straight through the waves we go.

Though the storm may give us hell, Straight through the waves we go.

To the sea where ancients fell; Straight to our graves we go.

"I'd almost forgotten about that one," Aldrnari said, feeling the redness growing on his cheeks. "Although I wasn't allowed out much, I wrote of what I imagined it would be like and what the others told me. I'm sure they embellished their tales, but I wanted to tell the stories—they kept my sanity."

Varn turned his gaze to the road in front of them. "There are some things I regret seeing since I left the security of my family. The isle of immortals is not without danger, but this world outside has grown worse. I'm sure you've noticed the threat looming in the skies."

"There's something off about those storms." Aldrnari tapped the heels of his boots on the bench. "With the state of the world, it helps to be in better company. Thank you for allowing me to be part of your crew."

Varn slapped Aldrnari's back. "It's nice having a normal human with us . . . as far as escaped pirates go."

"And there's nothing like having a famous poet immortalize our adventures after we've passed on," Jodoc said.

"I have been wondering," Aldrnari said to him and cleared his throat. "Is it okay for me to ask about the elves? Or are you related to the immortals?"

"Oh, I assure you, I am not related to our captain here." Jodoc laughed. "Yes, I belong to the race of elves and am loyal to our kingdom. It's not the first time an immortal and an elf have traveled together."

"Do you know of the old alliances?" Varn asked.

Aldrnari shook his head and leaned forward.

"The elves used to trade and live with humans. However, the fae warned of a disruption between the realms, and each became more cautious of the other. Treaties and borders kept their kingdoms apart. Eventually, the fae reached out to us immortals to intervene."

"His brother was an emissary between the fae and elves, after a human broke their treaty," Jodoc interjected.

"He was the wisest of us and could speak every language, often at once," Varn continued. "He helped keep the kingdoms from warring against each other, somewhat successfully."

"From what I've heard, the queen of the elves has restored trade and peace with humans," Aldrnari said. "I'm glad to have finally met one."

"We're like you." Jodoc tapped his nose. "With a little more understanding of the natural magic in the world. Some in my kingdom's inner circle say our queen learned fae magic. Hence the reason I'm interested in this festival. Imagine meeting a fae and conversing about such ancient teachings."

"I'd like to learn some spells," Aldrnari said. "Crowell used magic, but it was wrong. The creatures he summoned were fierce and full of an unnatural blood-lust."

"Keep in our company." Varn nudged him. "I'll show you some simple tricks. But enough of politics and magic. It's time for a grand entrance into the finest festival in the known lands. Let's see who and what we can find."

The walls around the city of Caetheal prevented entry from anywhere other than the main gate. Yet even in their height, they were dwarfed by the forest behind them. Aldrnari imagined the trees coming to life and swallowing up the town.

He laughed to himself while the crowds grew thicker. Guards inspected everyone's items in line and confiscated anything considered a weapon. A few warriors were allowed to carry theirs inside, if they kept them locked to their carts.

Some merchants gathered outside for the waiting entrants. The buzz of conversations and the noise of shuffled objects created a chaotic atmosphere.

Aldrnari's attention was caught by one table with a display of bottles. Each one held a micro scene of sand and shards of foliage around the water. The woman selling them wore a strange hat sculpted from different fish scales.

"Any port you can imagine is here," she said to Aldrnari. "I've traveled to nearly every port in the world. And emptied every bottle before filling it with soil from the land." She laughed as she sloshed the bottle she'd been drinking in front of him. "I'll sell you some of this too if you like. This one is mine, but there's plenty more under here. I make it myself."

Her breath smelled like it could light a fire, causing Aldrnari to lean back. He wished he hadn't made eye contact with her. Jodoc managed to pull him away and nodded to the woman.

"Ah, a man of the cloth," she said. "My apologies."

"None taken, miss." Jodoc smiled at her as they continued to the front of the line.

She shouted back at them with a comment about an elven monk, but Aldrnari ignored her.

After revealing the sparse contents of his bag and opening his vest to show he carried nothing harmful, the guards let him pass. It took Varn a while longer to get the cart with their supplies through.

"You know, without the added security, we could have walked in right away," Aldrnari said more to himself.

"Aye, but there will always be those unsavory types who want to start fights in the crowd." Varn shook his head. "It's one of those realities of the world we try to quell on our island. None can avoid the evil desire in those who thirst for power."

"Is that what happened to your brother?" Aldrnari instantly regretted letting his question slip out.

Varn stared off in the distance before answering. "The brother I'm trying to find is pure at heart. He never lost his childlike innocence. Others before him left with ill intent." He sighed and grabbed a map from one of the stalls. "We should head there." He pointed out an area on a steep hill. "It will be the best place to keep an eye on the gate and the perfect vantage point for us to spy a fae."

"How will we see them?" Aldrnari wondered aloud. "I was told they could become invisible or disguise themselves."

"They can," Jodoc said and pulled up his hood to maneuver through the gathering crowds. "Which makes it a bit more difficult to find them. They are documented to be part of a different realm altogether—appearing when they are needed."

"Then why would you look for one?" Aldrnari sighed at the futility of the elf's pursuit.

"For those who don't know how to recognize their magic, it may sound impossible," Jodoc muttered something under his breath, and his face changed from a bearded elf to a young woman. "Do I look like a monk?" He blew a kiss before changing back.

Aldrnari burst out laughing. "No. Although I'm not sure of the rules about women or elves in monasteries."

The three weaved around the masses to the spot Varn had suggested. There was something about being around an immortal Aldrnari couldn't quite place. He didn't mind leaving one captain to follow another with a more noble pursuit. Even if his companions enjoyed watching the festival instead of experiencing it.

6

Aldrnari quietly observed the crowds with Varn and Jodoc until his restlessness could no longer hide.

"Do you mind if I go on my own?" he asked them. "I'd like to see more of the festival up close."

"Explore to your heart's content," Varn said. "I wondered how long before you'd ask. I've been an observer for a long time and can sit for days. I sensed your spirit has a bit of wanderlust in it."

"There are such wonderful scents from the food, and we passed some interesting vendors. I won't be long." Aldrnari stood up and stretched.

"We'll set up our camp here." Varn handed him the map with his finger on the location. "Take this with you in case you lose track of time. It's easy to do in this sort of place. But don't expect us to have your tent set up."

"Thank you," Aldrnari said as he stuffed the map into his pouch. "I hope you find your brother."

"May the light guide you," Jodoc said with a smile.

Aldrnari rushed to the closest food vendor. The smell of smoked meats drew a long line. He waited patiently until realizing the coin he carried was the special one from Varn. With a growling stomach, he sought out other amusements to keep his mind preoccupied.

He didn't have to wander far. A young girl played a tin whistle to the people who passed by the potter's shop. Her hair was tied back into an intricate braid. Some gave a few coins as she nodded to the hat next to her.

Although younger, Aldrnari was certain she was an elf like Jodoc.

"My sympathies to your king," one of the nobles commented before placing some rare gems down.

The girl nodded soberly. She switched to a delicate tune and let the notes hang in the air before harmonizing them into a melody.

Aldrnari found himself leaning against a nearby tree, mesmerized by the sound and skill of the musician. He reached into his pouch and pulled out the silver coin. In the back of his mind, he questioned if Varn spoke the truth about it multiplying.

The elven girl's face lit up with a smile when he handed it to her. She bowed and trilled a few happy notes. Keeping an eye on him, she backed slowly to the potter's shop.

Aldrnari glanced away, hoping she didn't notice his embarrassed grin.

When he turned back, she was already further down the road, playing her songs to others in the lanes.

Aldrnari noticed his silver coin and the gems in the potter's tip jar.

"That was some fine playing," Aldrnari said, approaching a man sitting behind a table at the front of the shop. "I didn't know a tin whistle could make those sounds."

"I'm sorry," the potter said with a confused look. "What did you say about tin whistles?"

"The girl who was here playing."

"Oh, I didn't recognize you," the man grabbed a small cup and took a drink. "Were you here last year?"

"Well, no. This is my—"

"She could play like the angels," the man interrupted and wiped away a tear. "It's so hard without her. You probably don't want to hear it."

"I'm not sure what you are saying." Aldrnari raised an eyebrow. "I thought an elven girl was playing outside your shop."

"This is the first year my daughter is not with me," the man said and took off his hat, revealing slender ears. "I got up early this morning to work on her hair for the festival. Then I remembered. Sometimes it feels like she is here. With my king getting worse, I often hear the lament she liked."

He hummed the dirge she played moments ago.

Aldrnari looked down the street to see if he could catch sight of her again, but she must have turned down another. The girl or spirit didn't seem malicious. Perhaps she continued to help her father after passing from the physical realm.

While the old elf continued to hum, Aldrnari wandered into his shop. The handmade items were masterfully done with sturdy components. It was easy to see through the empty maze of shelves, but twisting around them without bumping into the more expensive vases proved to be a difficult task.

He nearly ran into someone crouched behind the bottom shelving.

"Please forgive me," he said. "I didn't see you there at first."

The girl's eyes met his, and he gasped. They were like the infinite gaze of the immortal's but deeper and sparkling. Colors of emerald green and a brilliant sapphire shifted in the light, causing a glow deep within her.

"You can see me?" she asked quietly. "I mean, why wouldn't you see me? I'm a normal person like you. Well, not that you're normal. You must be extraordinary to be able to see me. I think you're beautiful."

Her silken white cheeks reddened as she covered her mouth. From what Aldrnari could tell, they were the same age. Her pointed ears were smaller than an elf's and stuck out slightly from her long golden hair. She brushed the strands from her face, giving out a sweet aroma of a fresh garden.

Aldrnari tried to speak but being around her felt like waking in the morning light. He ran a hand through his hair and accidentally hit his feathered cap. His heart rate quickened as she stood up.

"I'm Mavelley," she said, not seeming to have any strain on her muscles from standing. It was almost like invisible strings had lifted her. "I must be honest, I've never had this happen before. How is it you see me and hear me? Wait, maybe you cannot hear me. You are the most handsome human I've seen."

"My name is Aldrnari," he said and cleared his throat. "I'm sorry I didn't say before. Thank you."

"Oh, you did hear me." She bit her lip and blushed again. "There's a code I must follow, but you've somehow broken it. I can't lie to you. I'm from the forest of the fae."

"I could sense something different about you," he said too suddenly. Her smile dropped slightly. "What I mean to say is, I've never met anyone like you. Human or fae, your beauty is enrapturing. I've written countless poems of love, but none of them come close to what I see in you."

"Did you find something you like in there?" the elf at the front of the shop called back to him.

"What?" Aldrnari noticed the potter staring in confusion.

"He can't see or hear me," Mavelley giggled. "Not yet anyway."

"Everything in here is quite lovely," Aldrnari said and winked to Mavelley.

"Let me know if you need help finding anything," the elf said and leaned back in his chair to continue humming.

"Do you like pottery too?" Mavelley asked. "I like to stop in here when I can. I stayed longer in previous years when his daughter was with us."

"Was she able to see you?" Aldrnari whispered.

"Sometimes I'd let myself be seen and play games with her. I sensed her spirit moments before you arrived. Maybe that's how you saw me."

"Whatever happened, I'm glad it did."

The beauty of the fairy before him disrupted every romantic prose he had written or read. It was as if every one of them belonged to her, and at the same time, he could never compose enough to express his feelings. He knew the potter would eventually become suspicious if he stayed in the shop all day, but he didn't want to leave her side.

"May I ask how long you were planning to stay here?" Aldrnari straightened his vest.

"Here?" She looked around like the question was new to her. "Oh, this shop. I hadn't meant to be here so long. The joust is supposed to be starting, but I don't want to leave unless you'll go with me."

Aldrnari felt like his heart would leap from his chest. He held out a hand to her and bowed as she placed her warm palm on his. The air around him filled with a flowery scent.

"Which one is your favorite?" he asked, pointing to the drinking vessels on the shelf in front of them.

"I've always liked this one," she said and picked up a simple mold with an intricate cord woven around it to create a handle.

He took it gently and led her to the front of the shop.

"Hello, young miss," the elf said with a nod to Mavelley. "I'm sorry I didn't notice you come in. Will this be everything for you today?"

Aldrnari set the porcelain mug on the table and reached into his pouch. The clanging of two coins put his mind at ease.

"Is this enough?" he placed one of them next to the mug.

The elf's eyes lit up. "I haven't seen a coin like this before. It must be rare." He squeezed the silver between his hands and held it up. "It's real enough for sure. Thank you, good sir."

"You're very welcome," Aldrnari said. "We want to see the joust next. Do you know when it starts?"

"Soon, so you best hurry." He motioned for them to lean in. "I know of a secret place you can watch it away from the crowds. Follow the path behind these shops. There's a food vendor right before you get to the stairs, near a portcullis, in case you're hungry. Take the stairs along the castle wall until you get to the locked tower and exit on your left. The path will take you up a hill on the far side of the grounds. There's also a small grove of trees young lovers like to stroll through before dusk."

"Well, we're not—" Aldrnari looked at Mavelley. "I mean, are we?"

She smiled sweetly. Her arm wrapped around his waist and pulled him closer.

"Thank you for your kindness," she said to the merchant. "We will look for this place. May your shop be blessed."

The elf nodded and quickly grabbed her hand with both of his. "I remember you. I can't begin to express how grateful I am for your presence. My daughter talked of you often. She spoke the truth when others didn't believe her. There were times I was convinced I saw you as well. Now I am certain. Go in grace and peace."

Mavelley bowed, and the two left the shop to seek out the secret grove.

7

Aldrnari stopped to get food for Mavelley and himself. As Varn had warned him, the silver coin did not duplicate when he bought the mug from the elven potter. He pulled out the remaining one and reluctantly gave it in exchange for a bag of food, knowing it would be the last use of it.

Any regret was worth the opportunity to spend more time with Mavelley. She seemed to produce her own light as they entered the enclosed staircase leading up the wall. They ascended through the tunnels by the potter's directions and found themselves in a small garden overlooking the festival grounds. A tree canopy covered the upper terrace, but brilliant flowers and small plants continued to grow underneath.

"I know this place." Mavelley touched one of the petals like she was trying to recover a memory. "My sisters and I helped make it."

"It's splendid," Aldrnari said, more enthralled with her.

"Look!" Mavelley pointed down to the row of guards stepping onto the field. "The human royalty is coming to the joust."

A blast from a trumpet was followed by cheers below. Light reflected off the glittering crowns of the king and queen, who stepped out from behind two oversized chairs. They waved for the audience to be quiet.

"Welcome one and all to the grand festival of Caetheal," the king announced and held up his hands. The crowd erupted again before he continued. "We want to start by giving a toast to the founders of this event who helped rebuild this city. Raise your glasses and give a cheer." Aldrnari couldn't make out the founder's names as the crowd shouted and clanked their bottles together. "If your feet find themselves pointed to Raikrune, be sure to browse their collection of rare books. You will be thrilled at what you discover. And speaking of thrills, we are nearly ready to announce your champions today. In this contest, humans, elves, and even the fae are welcome to participate—if they ever decide to leave their forest again."

"I'm not sure what he means by that," Mavelley said playfully and nudged Aldrnari.

"They'd better watch out if you joined the competition." He winked at her and squeezed her hand gently.

The commotion on the field drowned the rest of the king's speech. Knights rode out and battled against one another. Each strike of the lance to armor shook the air, drawing gasps from the crowd.

Aldrnari overlooked the time slipping by as the tournament lasted most of the day. Mavelley's gasps for the losers and cheers for the victors kept the event engaging. It wasn't until their food and drink dwindled to the last remnants that she stood to stretch.

"We should explore this area while it is ours alone," she said. "Follow me."

She took off through the flowers without him, and he had to run to catch up.

The vivid green of the grass lit up with thousands of fireflies. They swirled around her and sparkled in the trees above. Aldrnari couldn't deny his desire for her but felt unworthy to be in her presence—a brilliant fae should not be with a human like him.

They continued to chase each other through the small grove. Each streak from a firefly and scent from the disturbed flowers filled him with more love for Mavelley. Her iridescent wings carried her gently to a perfect ring of roses. There she sat with crossed legs and waited for Aldrnari to join her.

"I want to write songs and poems about you, but I don't think I have enough words," he said as she stared back into his eyes.

"Please try." She smiled. "I want to know what you think of me."

Aldrnari looked around at the fireflies illuminating the golden strands of Mavelley's hair. He recited the words as they formed in his mind.

If every star on a clear night
Shattered upon this gentle field,
They would dim in your wondrous light,
For your beauty is not concealed.
It shines out of the purest heart
That entices my own to stare,
Knowing our souls could never part
Even if the stars lose their glare.

"Oh my dearest, your poem was beautiful," she said. "I wish to hear more of your poetry and cannot express how grateful I am to be your muse."

"I feel like you are more than an inspiration." Aldrnari's cheeks warmed. "Since I've revealed my soul, can you tell me more about yourself? I want to learn about the fae and why most people can't see you."

"Others can't see us because we don't belong to this world." She placed her hands behind her and leaned back. "Although we can enter this realm, there's a chance it will disrupt the harmony in our forest, which isn't necessarily a bad thing. I've always enjoyed changing traditions."

"You sound quite rebellious. Should I be concerned?" He raised an eyebrow and laughed.

She tossed a handful of petals at him. "You've nothing to fear unless you try crossing into my realm. I keep most of our rules, but my heart has its own will—which is how I ended up here. When my sisters and I found out about this festival, we snuck out without our mother's permission. I can tell she's curious about it. I think she's afraid of the repercussions."

"What's so bad about interacting with humans?" Aldrnari teased.

"Years ago, a young human entered our forest and unlocked a dark force. It created fragments between the realms—particles of energy, draining the walls between our worlds." Mavelley's expression turned somber. "It keeps getting worse."

"If I understood more about magic and the hidden worlds, I could help you." Aldrnari placed his hand on her knee. "My friends follow the light as well. Maybe we could talk to them together and get their insight."

"I'd like that, although the hour is growing late." She glanced at the forest. "I wish the darkness hadn't come to us."

"I don't know how anyone could be tempted by it after being in a fae's presence, especially yours. I want to stay with you even after all lights blink from existence."

"If I could convince my mother to let me be with a human, I'd run away with you this instant," Mavelley said as she placed her hand on top of his. "But she believes a curse follows any fae who decides to leave their realm."

"Then maybe I'm meant to be part of your forest. The light must have brought us together for a reason. How else am I able to see you?"

"You are all I want to see," Mavelley said in a soft voice. She looked down at the festival below them. "My sisters will be searching for me. I should find them before they see us together. I'll return tomorrow. Will you be here?"

"I will." Aldrnari took her fingers lightly into his palm. "May I kiss your hand before we depart?"

Mavelley nodded and stepped toward him. He pressed his lips to her milky fingers. His heart felt like it had expanded within him—every whisper of love he could imagine filled it.

Her floral scent entered his nostrils as he breathed in before moving back.

"I hope to find you in the morning," Mavelley said with a loving smile. "If the light allows, we will never have to part again. Farewell, sweet poet."

Aldrnari watched her as she slipped away. Her wings let out a slight glimmer and lifted her above the trees to her forest.

He pressed his fingers to his mouth, taking in the last notes of her perfume before returning down the staircase. Everything seemed like a dream as he stumbled back onto the main streets.

"There you are," Jodoc said as he rushed up to meet Aldrnari.

He had entered the area where Varn marked their camp on the map, but no tents were set up.

"We wondered where you went," Jodoc continued and had to catch his breath. "We hoped nothing bad happened to you. This place is not safe."

"Why? What happened?" Aldrnari put a hand on Jodoc's shoulder to try to calm him down.

"We found them—the fae. Two of them, actually." Jodoc's eyes opened wider. "They are dazzling but dangerous. They said they were looking for someone, and I asked if they knew anything about Varn's brother. But that's about as far as I got with them. Once they discovered Varn was an immortal, they grew hostile like he was someone else."

"Oh no." Aldrnari panicked and looked back to the terrace. "Did they take him? Where is he?"

"We convinced them to leave, but Varn feared they would return once they found their sister. We had to set up camp down the road, outside of the festival grounds."

Aldrnari wanted to tell Jodoc about Mavelley, but the elf had already turned to run toward the gate. It took a few extra strides to keep up with him, but Aldrnari continued without stopping until they reached the camp. His tent had been set up already by the other two.

"Glad you made it back safely," Varn said, slipping out of the canvas structure. "I wanted to leave right away but figured you'd like to come with us. We hadn't made a formal offer for you to join our crew."

"Thank you for waiting," Aldrnari said. "I do want to join you and Jodoc."

"Great. We'll leave at first light. The fae said something about an immortal causing destruction in his wake. Hopefully, it was not my brother. I didn't see him down here, so we'll need to head back to Northeal."

"We can't go yet." Dread of breaking his promise to Mavelley made Aldrnari's voice tremble. "The fae won't attack us here. They're not allowed outside their forest." He cleared his throat. "I also met one. She is beautiful."

"Why didn't you tell me you met one?" Jodoc huffed. "We could have reasoned with her instead of rushing to get here."

"Trust me," Varn said and glared at Aldrnari. "They do not want us interfering with their affairs. The warning was not an idle threat. We need to leave here as soon as possible."

"Please captain, let me stay one more day," Aldrnari pleaded. "I gave my word to meet her tomorrow, and I fell in love with her. It goes beyond my dreams to imagine she feels the same way, but it's true. She wasn't supposed to be seen. I saw her when no one else could. It had to be fate or the light bringing us together."

"There seem to be greater forces at work," Jodoc said and held out his hands for everyone to sit again. "I sense you did not arrive in our company by accident. You spoke of a beggar, who we believe to be Varn's brother, and he told you to come to the tavern where we were staying." He turned to Varn. "He's probably behind this. We shouldn't let the lad go out on his own again."

"You could be right," Varn said, resting on a fallen log. "My brother had a knack for putting himself in opportune places when things were growing dark."

"What would you do if you were in my position?" Aldrnari asked. "If it's too risky for you, I can stay behind and meet up with you back in Northeal. I could talk with Mavelley, the fae I met, about the threat. Honestly, I hope she can come with us." He sat next to Varn. "Have you ever been in love before?"

"Aye, there's a long story to that question," Varn said and tossed a few chunks of wood into a heap. "It's best told around a good fire. I suppose I'll spare you some of the details. It was such a long time ago. Probably during the time of your great grandfather, when I was closer to your age."

Varn went on about how he fell in love with one of the women from his isle, but she journeyed away and found a mortal husband. His story was intriguing, but Aldrnari couldn't stop thinking about Mavelley. He hoped he could be like the mortal who was graced with meeting a forbidden love.

Something pulled inside of him like ropes, binding him to the fae. If he stopped loving her, he would cease to exist. He weighed the consequences of entering the fairy forest.

"Love is worth the risk," Varn concluded and stared into the fire. "I wish I had followed it back then."

"I'll go with you to the festival," Jodoc said and stretched out his legs.

Varn turned to Aldrnari. "Don't lose your senses around a pretty face. I'm going to rest so I can be up early. Keep it quiet."

Aldrnari nodded.

"She's not just a pretty face," he whispered to Jodoc after Varn disappeared into his tent. "If you met her, you'd know why I feel the way I do. We are meant for each other."

"I believe you." Jodoc covered the fire with dirt. "My king and queen fell in love at first sight. They were inseparable."

"Thank you." Aldrnari searched for the right words to say. "I'm not used to being trusted."

Jodoc patted him on the back and smiled. "Sometimes friends are closer than kin."

Aldrnari wondered if Varn would be willing to trust him. The next day would be glorious if he could see Mavelley again. In his dreams, he held her as she flew across the seas. Her wings lifted them above the clouds and shimmered in the moonlight of an endless sky.

8

An intricately woven green vest covered all but the flowing sleeves of his white shirt as Aldrnari prepared to meet Mavelley. His fashionable garments were accented by a velvet cap with an exotic feather sewn to the side. He would have liked to discover which bird produced it. In the back of his mind, he resolved to find out once he revisited the merchant to pay her back for the clothes—somehow.

The morning sun welcomed him into its warmth as he exited his tent. He had expected Varn's to be gone, but not Jodoc's. The elf wasn't there to greet him in his usual manner.

"Jodoc?" Aldrnari called out before spotting him at the far end of the camp.

The dark tones of Jodoc's hair and skin blended in with the trees, rendering him nearly invisible. If not for his recognizable robe, Aldrnari would have never guessed it to be his friend.

As he walked closer, he found Jodoc was not alone and had his eyes closed. The other two with him were male and female, holding hands. They all had their heads down with a somber expression.

Aldrnari caught some of what the female said about needing passage to the elven woods. She was also an elf, but the male appeared to be human.

"We will happily welcome your company, ma'am," Jodoc said and held a fist to his chest. "I'll speak with my captain. There is another soul who has recently joined our company. Speaking of." He beaconed Aldrnari closer. "May I introduce to you the parents of my queen?"

Aldrnari gave a clumsy bow.

"There are matters to discuss back on our ship," Jodoc said to him. "I should be watching you, but would you mind going to the festival on your own?"

Aldrnari nodded and cupped his hands together in an apology. "I didn't mean to interrupt."

The couple looked to be in distress. Streaks of tears caused a redness around their eyes.

"It's always a joy to be around new love, even in the darkest of times," Jodoc said and placed his hands around Aldrnari's. "Now, go find the one who captured your heart. We will be waiting for you at the Tide's Requiem. The matron of the tavern knows where it's docked," Jodoc smiled. "Light be with you."

"May your soul never decay," the queen's mother called out as Aldrnari turned down the path to the gates.

The number of guards near the entrance outnumbered the patrons standing in line. Aldrnari assumed most from the day before had camped inside the festival grounds. Judging from the number of boxes filled with weapons, the security diligently kept the area safe from any outside villainy.

"Halt!" one of the nearby sentries yelled out.

Aldrnari jumped back in alarm and looked around to see who was in trouble. Everyone else had cleared around him. The guard was pointing in his direction.

"You there, young man, step forward." The sternness in the man's deep voice caused Aldrnari to obey his command. "Where did you get that vest?"

"I—I received it as a gift from my father," he lied and unlaced the top. "Is it considered to be a weapon or something?"

"A merchant who makes the exact design claimed to have some of her wares stolen." The guard stomped toward him. "Let me see it."

Aldrnari crossed his legs and took a deep breath to gain control of his nerves. "Take it!"

In one fluid motion, he tossed the garment into the guard's face and rolled to the ground.

As he fled, he grabbed fistfuls of dirt, throwing them into the eyes of the other men who scrambled after him.

Boxes toppled as he sprinted around the outside wall. Enough cover of trees and shrubs allowed him to disappear into the foliage. The shouting from the guards slowly faded while he stalked through the overgrown forest.

The terrace overlooking the festival had to be nearby. He could tell by the flowers spilling over the edge of the wall. The soft bark of the ash trees reminded him of Mavelley's delicate skin as he searched for one to climb. They had all been cut back too far away to attempt a jump. Without the use of a long rope or ladder, it was useless.

As he continued toward the mighty trees, his thoughts twisted in confusion, and an overwhelming urge to turn back came over him. A fae couldn't have possibly fallen in love with a human. It must have been his imagination.

Aldrnari pulled some of the grass from the ground and rubbed it between his fingers. Its aroma produced a different scent than the plants he was accustomed to. It smelled sweeter and lighter than the ground he remembered on the terrace. A sense of loss filled him. He needed to leave.

He started to wander toward Caetheal when an object under his foot cracked from his weight. Shattered fragments of clay pottery stuck into the soft earth—the mug he bought for Mavelley.

A fog lifted from his mind, and he remembered their time on the terrace. Although he wondered how the pottery came to be at the edge of the forest, it was exactly what he needed to snap him back to the truth about their love. An invisible force guided him, pulling him forward.

He closed his eyes to recall Jodoc's requests from the light.

"Help me find her," he prayed for the first time. "There is a higher purpose for us to be together. I can feel it."

Although hidden to him before, the sunlight between the leaves revealed a magical barrier in his path. Getting into the fae's realm was more difficult than he imagined.

He looked down to the broken pottery as it reflected a brilliant white from its glazing. The spotted light from the fragments lingered in his eyes and resembled Mavelley's form, moving in the direction she departed from him. A slight passage opened through the magical safeguards.

"Thank you for guiding me," he exclaimed.

Aldrnari thought of when he first saw her when no one else could. Whatever magic the fae used created a residual trace he could follow. It was like an afterglow from a reflection.

He continued to focus on the area where Mavelley vanished. A sense of peace fell upon him, and he placed his feet in the dim streaks of light along the ground. In his mind, he imagined stepping through a surface sparkling with tiny fireflies. Each one grew warmer as he stepped closer, and a breeze blew through his hat, almost knocking it from his head.

The trail ended where thorns and vines wrapped the trunks of the trees tightly together, forming a wall none could squeeze through. A strange substance oozed from the bark.

Curiosity took the better of him, and he stretched out his hand to the liquid covering the trees . . . until something stirred beside him.

The rustling made him nearly stumble off the trail.

A soft chirping rang out from the bushes. Aldrnari smiled at the nearby bird when it hopped onto a branch. He recognized the long tail feathers as it ruffled them and chirped again.

The bird turned its head like it was smiling back at him. Flapping to lift back into the air, it flew between the trunks like they didn't hinder the creature at all.

Although faint, a trace of magic allowed Aldrnari to reach the area the bird had entered. From further away, the bark gave an optical illusion of a singular tree. Leaning closer, he discovered there were two, with one bent slightly forward. Their thorns were not covered in the sticky substance, and all pointed inward.

The jagged vines lessened as he pushed deeper into the strange tunnel. He had to squeeze sideways through the entrance until it widened enough for him to regain a normal posture.

It became more challenging to distinguish a clear path as each step illuminated under his boots. Pulses of light like waves across the sea rippled toward him. He wanted to step back but allowed it to scatter around the glow from his footsteps, creating a new rainbow of colors.

Aldrnari's heartbeat pounded while he pushed forward into the radiant forest. Every plant and tree root surged in brilliant displays with a life force of their own. His mind spun in their luminosity and fragrant aromas—like walking through a childhood dream.

A blinding flash caused him to cover his eyes as he stumbled away from the rippling waves of light. The sounds of the forest diminished, like the entirety of it was holding its breath.

His clamoring steps intensified his worry of alerting whatever defenses were in place, but he had to keep moving.

He wandered into an eerie part of the woods, where darkness seemed to be overtaking the trees. Dread replaced his wonder. It crept down his back and sent shudders through his spine. An absolute and overwhelming sensation leaked out its evil menace—like a gateway into another realm.

"We know what you desire," a ghastly voice whispered in Aldrnari's mind. *"What you seek can be found if you step closer. Only the worthy can enter. You can free us, and we shall free you into our power."*

Aldrnari shook his head. He instantly recognized the lies of power the voice promised. Its dark lure reminded him of being on the Stormeye. For too long, he trusted Crowell's empty words. They got him nowhere.

Aldrnari no longer cared what guarded the inner realms of the fae. He needed to follow the light and find Mavelley. The mysterious voice affirmed his determination.

Retracing his footsteps, he hurried back through the trees. Their bright colors brought back a calming sensation he desperately needed. He stopped to catch his breath and blinked to help his eyes adjust to the plants' vibrant glow.

"You shouldn't be out in the open," someone said in a hushed voice.

Aldrnari turned around to find the speaker, but there was none.

Another person responded, but he couldn't make out what they were saying. It was further down the path.

"I understand you are not mortal," the first person spoke again as Aldrnari crept closer to the sound.

Two men were crouched down in a small opening between the rows of trees. One of them appeared to be a fae and hovered off the ground. The other one looked to be a familiar beggar—Varn's brother.

"The tree was sealed once we found the human releasing them," the fae said and crossed his arms. "The elves took care of the other rupture. What do you mean there's a door to everywhere and nowhere?"

Varn's brother replied in his unknown tongue while the fae's eyes grew wider.

"This cannot be the work of the Nox—"

A hand yanked Aldrnari into the bushes and covered his mouth.

Mavelley sat facing him.

Aldrnari smiled as she moved her hand away. He wanted to speak of the love bursting from his chest, but she put a finger up to her lips.

Grasping him gently, she crawled under the branches of a large pine tree. Its heavy needles created the perfect shade to hide. Inside the cave of sticks, her pale skin reflected the dim light.

"How did you find me?" Aldrnari whispered at last.

"I was at the festival, and you weren't there," her voice wavered. "I figured something must have happened. But then, a longing inside of me led me back to my trees. All of us have a connection to our forest, and I could sense it was you. It shouldn't be possible for a human to enter without causing alarm, especially with all of our precautions. Are you sure you are human?" She gave him a wink and blushed at her flirting.

"Who's to say what any of us are?" Aldrnari placed his other hand on her cheek. "All I know is we need to be together. I've never been so certain of anything in my life."

"I feel the same." She leaned forward. "You may kiss me if you like."

Aldrnari pressed his lips to hers. Their warmth ignited a fire within him. He felt like the energy of the forest was exploding from them.

As he leaned back and opened his eyes, he discovered there were trails of light shooting out from their hiding place.

"We must leave," Mavelley said suddenly and squeezed his shoulders. "They know we are here."

She lifted him to his feet before he could protest. Pine needles stabbed his hat, and he had to brush them off after they exited the tree's cover.

"Is there another place we can go here?" Aldrnari asked, not wanting to leave the forest.

"It's not safe. The guardians will find us. I can explain more later. Run with me. They'll spot us if I fly." She jogged down the path.

Aldrnari had to use all his energy to keep up. The two of them raced toward the wall, almost exactly where he had entered.

"I'm not sure I'll be able to make it," Aldrnari said. "Can we fly over?"

"Not if you want to see me again," Mavelley said. "The others know our forest has been breached."

She stopped at the wall and closed her eyes.

"What does that mean for us?" Aldrnari placed his hands on his knees to catch his breath.

"The captain of our guards was distracted by an immortal, but he'll have to respond soon. If I leave, it could mean banishment." She turned toward him. "I am willing to take that risk for you."

"We can travel together if you would be my wife." Aldrnari couldn't bear the thought of being without her. He knelt down and held out his hand. "Will you marry me?"

9

"I will marry you!" The words sang from Mavelley's lips, and her wings lit up like lightning across a starless night. "I should join your captain's crew until we can convince my family to marry here. There's a harmony between our realms, and it would be disrupted if we wed anywhere else."

"I'm sure my captain would be thrilled to have you join us," he said, trying to hold back his concern about the encounter Varn had with her sisters. "And if they don't, we can find another ship."

Mavelley whispered a spell to the trees near the tunnel Aldrnari found to enter. It widened enough so both of them could pass without touching any thorns.

Once they were on the other side, she turned back with a longing expression. Aldrnari knew leaving her home would be difficult, and the feelings of regret would not soon pass. He hoped it wouldn't take long for them to return and be married in the forest's light.

"You should know, the others in my crew are not human," he said and held her hand as they hurried down the path to the festival. "The captain is actually a brother to the person you saw back there. He's an immortal too."

"Are you serious?" Mavelley's fingernails pressed into his skin as she stopped. "I was told he didn't make it to Northeal."

"He's been there for a while." Aldrnari stroked her arm, trying to get her to relax. "I didn't think you knew Varn."

"Varn? Who's Varn?"

"He's my captain, the immortal. He was the one who helped me when I first arrived."

"Oh." Mavelley bit her lip and continued walking past him. "I'm not sure if they can be trusted, but I trust you."

Aldrnari caught up to her, playing with the light fabric of her sleeves. "This one is different. He's a thousand times better than the captain I previously sailed with, and his crew is faithful to the light. The elf especially follows it. His name's Jodoc, and he was excited to meet a fae."

"You have an elf on your crew too?" Mavelley giggled. "Don't tell me trolls are holding the cargo down for you."

"We're not that bad." Aldrnari nudged her with his shoulder. "I'm probably the black sheep of the fold."

"I doubt you're the worst, but you've convinced me it's safe enough." Mavelley smiled.

"Wait," he pulled her aside as they neared the festival gates. "We should go around this area. It might cause problems if too many people see you." The guilt of lying to her about the encounter with the guards caused him to sigh. "There's another reason we need to avoid the entrance. I'll tell you on the way to Northeal. I need to find a merchant up there too."

"If you're in any trouble, I can help you."

Aldrnari held her hand as they snuck beside the road. Her desire to be with him made every step they shared feel like the right path.

The Tide's Requiem sat precisely where the matron of the tavern told them it would be. Its unique wood gleamed a marbled white with silk sails, giving it a sleek look against the other vessels nearly twice its size. The masts were folded in half but appeared to rise and catch speed before anyone else would have their bearings straight. Carved half the length of the starboard was the ship's name. Out on the sea, Aldrnari imagined it would be nearly invisible against the clouds and waves.

"Maybe you should sneak on board while I distract them," he said to Mavelley. "From what they said about their encounter with your sisters, it might be better if I told them about you first."

"Good idea." Mavelley kissed his cheek quickly. "Tell me when I need to be seen."

Aldrnari had forgotten she could turn invisible to most people as she floated onto the ship. A simple rope gangway stretched toward the dock, making entry onto the vessel more daunting. Jodoc stood at the end with his focus in the opposite direction.

"Hello friend," Aldrnari called to him. "So this is the ship of an immortal? It looks a little small to me."

Jodoc placed a fist to his chest and bowed. "We do not travel in order to make a grand display. Stealth is key to our safety out on the seas. Especially with those who claim to rule it."

"I can understand."

Aldrnari thought back to the countless attacks on other ships from his former captain. Crowell had no mercy on the plunders from those who sailed into his sight. And those who resisted met his magical ability to summon creatures from the depths. He had become so dependent on the beasts, Aldrnari couldn't remember the last time the Stormeye's thunderous cannons fired.

"Feel free to climb aboard," Jodoc said. "I'm waiting for the others. The queen's parents who were with me before the festival require our services. Varn is also off somewhere. Those fae sought him out, and he had to hide for a while. I suppose there's a downside to having a recognizable pale ship at the harbor." He chuckled to himself while Aldrnari stepped onto the gangway.

"Mind your footing," Jodoc continued and pointed to the ropes. "We've been doing this for a while, and they can get the better of you if you're not careful."

"I practically lived in the nets." Aldrnari held his hands up and wobbled his feet. It was less stable than he predicted. His balance fell to one side, and he had to catch himself. "Okay, this is a bit flimsy."

Jodoc shook his head with a smile. "I'll be up there shortly to show you to the rooms."

Aldrnari nodded and took his time the rest of the way up. Slipping through the holes into the sea became more of a threat in his state. He had been walking with Mavelley most of the day. Her feet hardly touched the ground, but he felt every step.

It had taken them a while to find the clothing vendor and apologize for his theft. After Mavelley gave the woman a few precious stones from her forest, she let them go and keep what he had been wearing.

"It doesn't look like much up here," Jodoc said from behind him. "Below deck is quite comfortable."

Aldrnari followed him down wooden stairs that shifted from the elf's weight. Once they reached the bottom, Jodoc pointed out the captain's quarters. Its door was locked, not allowing any further inspection.

The low ceiling made Jodoc crouch through the narrow hallways. Once they reached the center, he stopped.

A tree had been carved onto a door frame. No windows or light entered the open room apart from what spilled in from the stairs. Aldrnari could make out shapes of books stacked in various piles on the floors and shelves.

"Sorry, I forget about human vision sometimes," Jodoc said and whispered a spell that lit up the carvings.

Designs wrapped themselves into a cacophony of plants and exotic creatures along the walls. An owl spread its carved wings over the ceiling. In the dim light, it appeared to be watching the newcomer.

"These rooms do feel bigger than the top deck," Aldrnari said, trying to quell his fears. "Are there any with a little more lighting?"

"There are a few down the hall. Please save the largest one for our two guests." Jodoc turned to the stairs. "They might be close. I sense a presence nearby I can't quite place. Don't wait for me to get settled. I'll gather us some extra bedding while I'm out."

The elf left Aldrnari to wander alone through the lower deck of the ship. He was eager to find a room but more excited to locate Mavelley. She had to be hiding close by.

A slight glimmer from her wings lit the hallway before she emerged. In a flash of light, she flew to his side.

"I hope it's safe for me," she said, hugging him tightly. "I overheard your friend say others were coming. Hopefully, they are like him. He seems nice."

"He's the elf I was telling you about." Aldrnari held her a little longer. "I should've told him about you joining us."

"What? I figured that would be the first thing you did. How can we sail with them if they don't allow me to be on the ship?"

"It will be fine once they meet you." Aldrnari held her hand between his. "Please trust me. I'll see if they're back yet and tell them right away."

"Okay," Mavelley said with a softer tone. "Please don't be gone for too long. My heart is full when you are near, and I don't want to hide our love."

"I agree. If this works, we will know it's the light's will for us to be together."

"I already know it is." Mavelley leaned in close to whisper. "I dreamed of you before we met."

They kissed again before he parted to check above deck.

A dark thought danced in the back of his mind while he climbed the stairs. With how small the ship was fashioned, it could easily be piloted by one. He didn't need to wait for the others to return—Mavelley would certainly understand if he left without them.

The breeze caught a loose flap of the topsail and caused Varn's ship to rock gently.

It brought Aldrnari back to the serene feeling he experienced stepping into the forest. His path needed to keep true to the light. And he had to admit, he was curious about how his crewmates would react when they found out about his stowaway.

It didn't take long for the familiar shapes of Jodoc and Varn to come into view. Their features towered over the common sailors at the dock. Aldrnari wondered if his willingness to trust them had more to do with their imposing physique than their charming personalities. He was glad he waited and didn't try to run away with their ship.

"So you decided to stick around?" Varn called out to him.

Aldrnari waved as a tightness formed in his chest. If they refused to allow Mavelley to travel with them, he didn't know what he'd do.

"I hope you don't mind the added company," Varn continued as he crossed the gangway. "There has been a sad occurrence, and we must set sail."

"I need to tell you something." Aldrnari took a deep breath and stepped back to allow Jodoc and the royal couple to climb up to the deck.

"Before you begin, let me explain the dilemma we are in," Varn said, making sure the rail was sturdy enough for him to lean against. "This is quite a serious matter. We found out the king of the elves has passed from the physical realm." He turned to the couple and gave a sympathetic bow. "Not only this, but the fae have accused me of terrible crimes. The search for my brother has to be shelved for the time being."

Aldrnari stepped forward to tell him what happened in the forest, but Varn put his hand up to stop him.

"Please, we shouldn't delay our voyage any longer," he said. "I need to take our guests to the elven woods. They are the queen's parents."

"I understand, sir," Aldrnari said and sighed. "You should know—"

"Did you see her again?" Jodoc interrupted him, placing a large bag onto the deck. "I'm sorry, but I must know. The ones we met before didn't remind me of those told in stories. They were once close to the elves, so I believed them to be more benevolent."

"The fae are more wonderful than any story could depict," Aldrnari said, closing his eyes to remember the forest. "This is what I want to tell you. I followed the light and found her again. I asked her to marry me, and she said yes."

"Congratulations." Jodoc rushed up to him, giving a hug that squeezed out his breath.

"How did you get her parents to agree?" Varn asked, crossing his arms.

"Well, I didn't exactly get to talk to her parents." Aldrnari took off his hat and looked away. "We were in a rush to get out of the forest when I asked her."

"You did what?" Varn boomed. "Are you mad? The fae will for sure be hunting us. They'll probably accuse me of kidnapping. I have an inclination to leave you here and get all of this sorted out."

"I don't think we can go back to the forest. Mavelley might have been banished."

Aldrnari couldn't understand Varn's response as he muttered in an ancient tongue. Jodoc covered his face with his palm.

"I know in my heart we are meant to be together," Aldrnari pleaded with them. "My love for her cannot be stilled. You would have to kill me first."

"That can be arranged," Varn said and unsheathed his blade.

Aldrnari's eyes grew wide as he stumbled back, trying to increase the distance between him and the immortal's menacing grin.

"Captain?" Jodoc blurted out. "Are you mad too?"

"I'm messing with him," Varn said and snapped his sword back in its place. "He made the offer."

"Let's talk about this." Jodoc motioned to the queen's parents, who appeared to be amused at the situation. "There are greater things at work here. I've sensed another soul watching us. She's here, isn't she?"

"What?" Varn's glare was more threatening than his blade.

Aldrnari thought he'd seen the same expression on Crowell during his former captain's fits of rage. The resemblance startled him to his knees.

"This is not the right way," the queen's mother spoke up in a melodic voice. "This human said he followed the light to meet her. Did it guide you into the forest as well?"

"It did," Aldrnari said, regaining his footing to stand. "Otherwise, I wouldn't have been able to pass through their wall of trees. Something led our paths together. I can't imagine it being anything other than the light."

"Love bridges the realms we often think impossible to cross," the queen's mother said and smiled at her husband. "Perhaps their bond will heal the wounds of the past between our people. We shouldn't be the ones to hinder the light of love."

"Forgive me for my outburst," Varn said in a softer tone. "I will not become like my other brother and be lured into darkness.

We have wanted to restore peace between the realms, and having a fae on our crew would be a blessing."

"Does this mean we can both travel with you?" Aldrnari asked and looked back to the stairs. "I can assure you she's not like the others you met. Once you see her, you'll know it too."

"Much like the immortals." Jodoc nudged Varn.

"You speak the truth, and you are both welcome here," Varn said. "However, we need to set off before it gets too late. Bring her up."

"Thank you." Aldrnari let out the breath he'd been holding in. A jarring thought crept up on him and caused him to turn back. "Sorry to be a bother. I know we were looking for your brother, but you just mentioned one another who followed a darker path. What is his name?"

He wanted to be wrong but knew what Varn would say before the words escaped from his lips.

"Crowell."

10

The voyage to the elven woods took longer than expected as increasing storms blocked the main routes. Varn allowed Aldrnari to take over the charting of their course. With a new map, he marked off the areas no longer safe to cross and ones he knew Crowell liked to use. It helped him focus on the destination and not that he was sailing with the brother of his former captain.

Being with Mavelley also put Aldrnari's mind at ease. It made him wish he could have saved his book of poetry. A blank collection of papers would suffice as a myriad of new lyrics filled his mind.

Aldrnari recited each poem he recalled on their journey, hoping she would help him remember them when he had a new book.

"Steady on," Varn called from the helm. "I spy our destination ahead."

Aldrnari had been gazing into Mavelley's eyes and had lost track of how close they were getting.

"Should I be concerned about our arrival?" he whispered to her. "I know the feelings between humans and elves are tense."

"If anyone tries to give you grief, they'll have to go through me," she said and gave him a wink.

"Your beauty can stop my heart. I can't imagine what would happen if someone got on your bad side."

She squeezed his hand, and he led her to the bow. Jodoc had his back against the rail like he'd been expecting them.

"It will be nice to see my family again," he said. "Although, I sense much has changed in the last few days. I'll go wake the royals."

Doubt crept up on Aldrnari as Jodoc proceeded to the stairs. The elf remained a mystery to him. In his eagerness to be with Mavelley, he neglected to converse much with the rest of the crew.

"Have you seen many elves before?" Aldrnari asked her.

"Honestly, nothing more than watching them at the festivals. Your friend is the first I've spoken with, and he keeps to himself. I hope I don't intimidate him or anything."

"My guess is he's broken up about the king's death." Aldrnari watched the waves part from the front of the ship. "I noticed his mood getting darker. My former crew mocked the elves for having their king marry a half-human. Some joked about finding an elf of their own to seduce. I'm surprised we didn't have any on the Stormeye, if Crowell is an immortal."

"What did you say?" Mavelley backed away suddenly. "Crowell was your former captain?"

Aldrnari gave her a puzzled look. "Yes. He was the one I escaped from. They kidnapped me at a young age and forced me to stay on the ship."

"Oh, sorry," Mavelley said softly. "You mentioned your escape. I guess I didn't connect that it was from the Stormeye. It's unbelievable how someone so incredible could come from that horrid ship. All of my kind were warned about him. I'm glad he turned away from Northeal."

"It would have been a little easier for me to escape if he'd made it to port." Aldrnari put his arm around her. "But it sounds like it would have been worse for everyone else."

"He's been seeking out our magic to corrupt it for his sinister gain. From what I've learned, his abilities would bring a darkness we've desperately locked away."

"Is it his summoning powers? They always made me uneasy. I could tell they drew from an evil place. The creatures had a strange aura around them."

"There are certain doors which shouldn't be opened," Mavelley said sternly. "The guardians assured us nothing could unlock them again, but I'm worried he could find a way. Immortals are patient. They have to be."

She sighed and put her head on his shoulder. Her hair smelled of the enchanted forest. Aldrnari felt dizzy breathing it in.

"I won't let anything bad happen to you," he said and kissed the top of her head. "I wish we could be married now so you'd know how much I love you."

They held each other tightly as the ship approached the dock. Within moments, Varn had the gangway secured. It seemed odd to arrive and not be greeted by a harbormaster—or anyone. Aldrnari suspected they landed in a secluded area. Having the queen's parents on board might have been more treacherous than their captain wanted to admit.

"Get yourselves ready," Varn commanded. "Our escort won't want to delay our journey any longer."

Aldrnari took Mavelley by the hand and helped her cross the rope bridge. Her toes brushed the gangway slightly as she glided down.

The array of slender trees at the shoreline were bare of lower branches but produced broad leaves at the top. Movement among a small group of bushes caught Aldrnari's attention. If he wasn't looking in the right direction, it would have been impossible to see the soldier waiting for them. His hair and skin color blended in with the bark and leaves around him. A patterned robe camouflaged into the surroundings.

"Home," Jodoc said as he hoisted a small pack over his shoulder. "It never looks the same."

"If you will come with us, your highness," the elven guard said and bowed to the royals. "I fear our lodging situations may not meet your expectations. With the grave news, our people have gathered from many reaches of our kingdom. We did not expect this large of a company."

"As you are aware, Jodoc travels with an immortal." The queen's mother kept a stately composure. "And I'm certain my daughter will be especially interested in meeting this couple." She motioned to Aldrnari and Mavelley. "She is a fae, and this is her betrothed."

"In all my years." The guard's eyes went wide and filled with joyful tears. "You've no idea what this will mean to us. We must hurry before others see her." He took off his outer cloak and held it out to Mavelley. "Please wear this. Some could see your presence as a threat. Most of us believe your magic helped us defeat a great evil, but others blame you for the curse, which our queen saved us from."

"I understand," Mavelley said, pulling the cloak over to hide her hair and wings. "I am sorry for your loss."

The guard nodded and chuckled to himself. "So you are engaged to a human?"

"How could I not be?" She slipped her arm around Aldrnari.

He grinned and found himself at a loss for words.

"Love cannot be denied," the queen's mother said, stepping forward with her husband. "If it means leaving your home behind and bearing the scorn of your people, so be it."

"Apologies, ma'am." The guard held a fist to his chest and bowed again. "I wouldn't want you to think ill of me. Love's waters connect many lands together. Let us leave in haste."

Varn took the lead behind the guard. The rest of the crew followed through the giant trees. Their leaves were spread wide, despite the distance between each one. It gave plenty of room to travel in their shade. If Aldrnari hadn't seen the ones in Mavelley's forest, he would have viewed them as the most magnificent he'd beheld.

"We must be getting close," Jodoc whispered from behind him. "We're being watched."

"You're being listened to as well," a voice sounded above them.

The branches rustled as a figure dropped from the trees. The older elf landed in a crouched position. He nodded to the elven guard who had been their escort.

"It is good to see you again," the older one said to Jodoc and embraced the large elf. "I knew we could trust you to bring them here safely." He turned to the others and held a fist to his chest. "Light blessings to you as well. You arrived here as strangers, but let us be strangers no longer. I am Roparzh, cousin to Jodoc and captain of the queen's guard."

"I'm surprised to see you away from her," Jodoc said. "But I understand if she needs her solitude in grief. I hope she keeps her favor with our people."

"With King Llyros' passing, our kind is returning to the old ways of hatred for humans. She is safe for now, but we must return in haste." Roparzh stepped back. "Who might your friends be?"

"I'm sure you've heard of my captain, Varn," Jodoc said as the immortal tipped his hat. "This lad is Aldrnari, and he has a pure heart for a human. I hope you trust my judgment on this."

"Bringing the queen's father into our kingdom is risky enough," Roparzh said in a condescending voice. "A human with no ties to our woods could bring disaster."

Jodoc held up his hands to calm him down. "Once you learn who our other companion is, all doubt will be erased." He motioned for Mavelley to remove her hood. "This is his betrothed, one of the fae."

"You mean—really?" Roparzh raised an eyebrow and cracked a smile. "Interesting. If my mother were alive, she'd be welcoming you in without question. Forgive my hesitation."

"Thank you for trusting us," Aldrnari said and bowed. "I promise to follow whatever instruction is given to me in your kingdom."

"Don't be misled," Roparzh said and pointed up to the branches he descended from. "My company trusts humans less and will let their arrows fly before a threat is raised. We will not allow anyone to lift a weapon in our queen's presence. You're lucky I've been watching for your arrival and found you before one of my younger guards."

"We should be thanking the light for bringing us here safely," the queen's mother said. "It is more than luck."

Roparzh smiled and nodded. "I have a room prepared for you and your husband. However, there are not many to spare for the others." He turned to Mavelley. "Will you and the human be sharing quarters?"

Mavelley looked at Aldrnari with concern, waiting for him to respond.

"We're not married yet," Aldrnari said as his heart raced at the thought. "I mean . . . I want to save our intimacy until we are wed." He felt her hand gently squeeze his in agreement. "Is there room on the floor with Jodoc and Varn?"

"A wise choice." Roparzh tilted his head to the side. "I'm not certain there will be enough bedding for it, but there is space."

"I brought extra blankets with me," Jodoc said, holding out his bag. "And he's more than welcome to take my bed as I've matters to discuss with my family."

"Understood." Roparzh motioned to his soldiers in the trees, and a few climbed down. "Follow me closely to the inner circles. We should meet with the queen first."

The sudden realization he was going to be meeting with the queen of the elves made Aldrnari hop in line behind the guards. He knew nothing of them, other than what Jodoc mentioned.

Roparzh turned sharply into the woods while more patrols revealed themselves the closer they came to the elven fortress. A long row of trees bent toward each other to form the arched entrance. Their limbs twisted together into a roof as the company entered the spiraling tunnels of the elven city.

11

"I must ask you to wait here before we proceed," Roparzh said as they entered a small room before a set of massive doors. "The council has been in discussions over the reign of our queen. Help yourselves to a drink while I speak with them."

He opened the doors enough to slip inside and closed them quickly.

"Are we safe?" Aldrnari whispered to Jodoc.

"I hope so," he said, being the first to fill up a small cup from the slender container. "Let me do the talking when he gets back. My parents served on the council for a while." He sniffed the drink and tipped his head back while he threw the liquid down his gullet. "Refreshing, whatever it is. A bit too sweet for my taste."

Aldrnari took one of the cups from the side table, and Jodoc filled it up. He offered it to Mavelley first. She had a look of curiosity but motioned for him to try it.

Like Jodoc, he breathed in the sweet aroma lifting from the hot drink. It tasted of honey and infused herbs when he took a sip. His senses became alert to his surroundings.

The area appeared to be crafted from the trees, but not by hand. It was like the wood formed itself into ornate patterns and shapes with guidance from an outside force—elven magic.

There was a hint of sadness about the place with the recent loss of their king. The queen's parents had remained silent most of the trip, as did Varn. Aldrnari couldn't tell if the tension in the air or the stimulating beverage made his hands shake in anticipation.

"There's something strange about this tea," he said, holding it up to his nose again. "I don't know if it's intended for humans."

"Ah yes, I forgot to inform you of its magical properties," Jodoc said and poured a little more for himself. "People often overlook the hidden abilities of the elements around us. I'm sure Mavelley understands this. You see this world from another realm, don't you?"

"I do?" Mavelley asked and looked to the ceiling. "I suppose it is different for you. I've noticed the energy pulsing through the doors is weakening. Roparzh will be back soon."

Aldrnari could sense a hum of power being used further away from the wooden doors. He was surprised he didn't notice it sooner. The elves' security was similar to the magical barriers in the fae's forest.

The waves of energy grew still as Roparzh emerged from the other room. His movements were swift and precise.

"It would be wise for all of you to hold your tongue when we enter the chambers," he said with a stern glare. "The Circle of Sorcerers has also gathered within. We should keep the girl fae hidden for the time being—until we can meet with the queen alone. She wants to speak with her."

"Should we deceive our elders in such a way?" Jodoc asked. "Won't the Circle sense her presence?"

"They are distracted by other matters." Roparzh leaned in with a softer expression. "I fear what we once believed about the light has diminished. We would do well to keep our heads down."

Everyone did as he said and followed him inside the council chamber. The circular room was full of chairs, positioned near smaller tables. Each elf who occupied them talked above the noise of the other.

"Now we're allowing defilers in our inner sanctums," Aldrnari overheard one of them say as they walked past a group of elders.

Roparzh continued to lead them through the large arena toward a long black and red tapestry on the far wall. Its colors intertwined into an illusion of an owl perched above the room. The intricate weaving made the owl appear to be living and in wait for its next prey.

A semi-circle of high-backed chairs in front of it indicated the seating of significant members. Some had their eyes closed and seemed to be listening to everyone at once. They conversed in whispers to each other. In the center sat a white-haired elf whose robe wrapped around him several times to create a notable appearance.

"Grandmage, these are the ones which arrived at the queen's request," Roparzh said while bowing with a fist on his chest.

"Of course she would have them come at this time." The white-haired elf stood and sighed. "Katell is alone in her study. She has rooms near there for your stay. I suggest keeping an eye on that one." His bony finger pointed to Aldrnari. "We know

Katell's parents can be trusted, but this one has seen the darkness. I sense it in his presence."

Aldrnari felt Mavelley rub her hand across his back to comfort him.

"I will take responsibility if anything happens," Jodoc said, stepping forward. "You know my discernment is wise. It's part of the reason why I was chosen by—" His voice cracked, and he bowed his head. "Why King Llyros sent me with the immortal."

The Grandmage took his time to sit back in his chair. "The former king didn't make the best decisions."

"Katell," one of the elves near them sneered.

"Regardless, I know your family well. Your father is being considered to be the next crowned king. Do you plan to be with us long enough to see this pass?"

Jodoc looked to Varn before turning back to the Grandmage. "I will stay as long as we are welcome here. My family is loyal to the kingdom, but you know our history of service to the immortals."

"The youthfulness in your eyes tells me we cannot keep you for long. Your heart is at sea, like the others in your company. I hope when you decide to stay in one place, you will find it to be here." The Grandmage motioned to a door beside the tapestry.

"Katell is eager to speak with her parents. I should delay you no further."

"Beware the corruption," Jodoc said, holding his fist to his chest.

"May your soul never decay," the Grandmage muttered with reluctance.

Roparzh rushed the others to the door and was the first to enter. The dim light of the passage almost made Aldrnari run into those in front of him. If not for Mavelley's subtle glowing, he would have toppled over.

"Why did he point to me?" he whispered to Jodoc when they were far enough down the hallway.

"I may have underplayed the significant distrust us elves have toward humans," Jodoc said and shook his head. "The rift has gotten worse. It's a wonder we didn't meet more resistance. The Circle of Sorcerers tolerated outsiders by order of our former king, but I had prayed their hatred would have ended. I hope Katell is well."

"You have such a gift for seeing the best in people," Mavelley commented with a smile. "I hope you can bring your people back to the light."

"Coming from a fae, that means more than you'll know," Jodoc said. "My uncle worked closely with your kind and was tasked to observe their dealings in Caetheal. He also traveled with an immortal, right before the corruption hit our lands. So much can change over the years." He glanced at Roparzh. "We all remember his death."

"Quiet," Roparzh said and held his hand back to them. "Our queen is in mourning, and we are near her study. Let us be respectful." He carefully pulled back the curtain to the next room. "I will stay between here and the council to make sure you are not disturbed."

"Thank you," the queen's mother whispered.

"I have watched over Katell from the beginning as you requested. She needs you now." He bowed to her and parted the veil.

Aldrnari had to blink from the brilliant light in contrast to the dim halls. As his eyes adjusted, the rows of bookshelves overwhelmed him.

He imagined every written work to be stored in Katell's study. Antiquated tomes were piled in front of shelves stuffed full of crumbling scrolls. Each table had different sizes of books and maps scattered across them. The scent of aged paper urged him to explore.

Aldrnari nearly forgot about the others with him until Mavelley pulled him closer.

"It's her," she whispered and pointed out a figure on the ground within a ring of candles.

"Mother?" Part of the woman's face was revealed from under her dark robe. "Is it you?"

"Oh, my child," the queen's mother said and rushed over to her side.

"We came as soon as we could," her father said, following behind. "These are the ones who helped us reach your shores safely."

The queen looked up at them, and Aldrnari saw the features of both her parents in the woman. Her black hair had white streaks like her father's beard. The high elven cheekbones stood out in contrast to her round ears. With a tired expression, she curved her lips into a warm smile.

"Thank you for coming here," she said and turned back to her mother. "It has been too many years since your last visit, and it's been so hard without Llyros. I wish we could have brought you back before this happened."

"Katell, we have been with you and watching you from a distance. Your father and I thought it best to wait. The hatred the others have toward him did not leave as quickly as it rose."

"Love will be stronger," Katell said. "Llyros believed our kingdoms would be reunited and would have wanted me to keep strong. His passing happened so fast, and yet, we knew this day would come. He kept getting worse." A tear rolled down her cheek, and she brushed it off to stand. "Please forgive my state. A queen should be able to handle her emotions. Especially an elven one. Let me show you to your rooms."

She brushed her hair back while she pulled down her hood.

"Wait," she said and wiped her cheeks again. "I recognize the others' kind—even the immortal—but I have not seen one like you before. Your eyes." She stepped closer to Mavelley. "They are a wonder and yet a familiarity. Do you practice the spells of the light?"

"In a sense, I do," Mavelley said and took off the cloak she used to disguise herself. "I am Mavelley of the fae."

"You are?" Katell looked as if she couldn't decide to hug her or faint on the spot. "A fae traveling with a human and an immortal? This is incredible. I know the elves traveled with immortals, but I didn't know your kind left their forest except for times of extreme importance. Were you here when there was the rupture in our woods?"

"I'm much too young for those events." Mavelley blushed. "I am with a human because we are engaged."

"This one? Here?" Katell squinted at Aldrnari. "These are strange times indeed. I hope you don't mind, I wasn't able to secure many rooms."

"We have it figured out," Aldrnari said. "I can stay with Varn."

"Where will Jodoc stay?"

"Your highness," Jodoc said and bowed. "I would like some time to speak with my parents and stay with them if it pleases you. With their position on the council, I might be able to help with the diplomacy between the humans and elves."

"That would bring me great joy," Katell said. "Are there any other arrangements I need to be made aware of?"

Aldrnari noticed a slight challenge in her tone but couldn't hold back his curiosity. "Might I be able to stay longer in this room? I've never seen any place like this, and the books I wrote were lost. There are so many here."

He caught a glare coming from Varn and awaited a reprimand for his outburst.

Instead of anger, Katell burst into laughter.

"You are a strange one," she said, trying to hide her smile. "There's a bag near the door. Please fill it with any but the large one on the table. That one is special, from my mother." She turned to her and sighed. "Although I have it memorized, I'd like to keep it close."

"Thank you," Aldrnari said and headed for the bag she mentioned.

"Don't be too long," Mavelley called out to him as the rest of the crew followed Katell out the door.

He thought he heard the queen warning of certain books to avoid in the darker areas of the study. His attention had already become enthralled by the endless tales before him.

The mention of shadows drew him further down the shelves to the back of the room.

Orbs of light that illuminated the room became fewer as he explored. Dust trails from his finger across the leather covers created tiny particles in the haze. They tickled his nose while he breathed in stale air. It seemed heavy, like a presence took it from him.

His footsteps stopped at the end of the rows in a small enclave along the wall. One book sat behind crude and weathered bars. A few had fallen from the crumbled rock, trying to hold them in place. Enough of a gap allowed him to reach in.

"Closer," a voice whispered from inside the cage.

He quickly withdrew his hand and peeked inside. Except for the strange book, there was nothing but stone.

Katell's warning about the forbidden books seemed to writhe into his gut until a new desire overpowered his doubt. Something inside the pages wanted to be seen. Curiosity replaced his reluctance and assured him there would be no harm.

Aldrnari reached back in and wiggled the book loose from its restraints.

"Now, let's see what you hide," he said while wiping off the strange-looking tree on the cover.

Peeling it open, he found the pages to be completely blank. Not a drop of ink or stain graced the inside.

His first instinct was to put it back and pretend like he never broke it free from its forgotten area. Yet, a thought lingered in the back of his mind. It would be the perfect book for his poetry. No one would miss it, and he could fill it with his feelings for Mavelley.

Aldrnari lightly dropped the empty book into his new bag.

Without time for remorse, he hurried back to the main area of the room. More stories needed to join his acquisition, and it would be easy to lose days in the volumes of Katell's study.

12

Voices echoed into the guest room where Aldrnari had been asleep. The whispers remained inaudible, causing him to sit up. He crept into the hallway to see Jodoc speaking with Varn.

"I suppose we shouldn't delay them any longer," Varn said, glancing at Aldrnari. "You do what you must."

Jodoc bowed and turned to Aldrnari like he wanted to say something, but quickly departed down the darkened corridors.

"He's not good with goodbyes," Varn explained. "I've no doubt he will join us again soon." He tightened the strings wrapping around his shirt sleeves. "Things are worse than I feared. With the king's passing, the rest of the elves do not see Katell as fit to rule alone . . . or at all. Jodoc is trying to maintain peace with the humans, but your presence may jeopardize it. Plus, I know how eager you are to be married."

Aldrnari's emotions flashed between anger and embarrassment. He wanted to stay and help Jodoc, but if he could help the elves by leaving, he needed to trust Varn's judgment.

"Does Mavelley know?" he asked.

"She's with Katell in her study. They've been up for a while, sharing their knowledge of magic. The queen learned of fae spells in the past, and I assumed her fascination with them would spill out once we arrived. It's good to have the light in such dark times."

Varn held his hand out for Aldrnari to proceed first.

"Let me grab my gear." Aldrnari rushed back into the room to gather his new bag before returning to the study with Varn.

Mavelley and Katell were huddled over the table, flipping through various texts of ancient magic. Katell looked up first to the new arrivals.

"Speaking of the ones we love, here is yours," Katell said as she locked eyes with them.

"Aldrnari, I'm so glad you're awake." Mavelley rushed over to embrace him. The strands of her silken hair brushed against his neck. "I don't want to wait another day for us to be married."

Her words filled his heart as a thought caused him to lead her back to Katell.

"Can we get married here?" Aldrnari asked. "I know it's a difficult time, but we could bring joy to this place."

"We spoke of this," Katell said and leaned against a shelf of books. "I don't think the council will allow a human ceremony in our lands. And the realm of the fae must be in balance. I know love is stronger, but you should be wed properly."

"I wish you and Llyros had more time together," Mavelley kept one hand on Aldrnari and grabbed Katell's with her other. "In time, you will see each other again."

"Each day I had with him was more than I could have hoped for." Katell sighed. "Please travel with speed and safety. I sense a dark presence I haven't felt in a long time. I hope I'm wrong about it." She looked at Aldrnari carefully and pulled her hood back up as Varn cleared his throat.

Aldrnari held his bag closer. "Captain, is the ship ready for us?"

"Aye, we are set to sail," Varn said. "I trust there will be no qualms about us leaving early. I'm hoping my brother will show up in Northeal and would like to have him with us when we return." He knelt to Katell. "Thank you again for your hospitality.

A true queen welcomes the watchers. We serve the light and seek the betterment of those who follow. May the light bless you."

"And may your soul never decay," Katell responded and held a fist to her chest.

"Thank you," Aldrnari said and gave an awkward bow.

"We should get to the ship in haste," Mavelley whispered. "It won't be long until we can be together forever."

She squeezed his hand and led Aldrnari to the door. They waited outside while Katell spoke with Varn privately. Aldrnari didn't like the idea of retreating but hoped they would someday return to the elven kingdom as husband and wife.

"What were you talking to Katell about before we left?" Aldrnari asked Varn when they were a fair distance from the elven port and on the open sea. "She sounded a little eager to get us out of there."

"She's concerned about the veils, as we all are." Varn checked the ropes around the wheel again, making sure they were sailing true to Northeal. "They're the reason why I left my island. My brothers sought answers first. One of them found a way to draw out creatures from them. I'm not sure why he desired the power. We know of its corruption on the casters."

"From what I know of Crowell, he cares nothing about his sanity. I'm surprised you two could be related. You don't resemble him in the slightest."

"I've heard stories of him merging with some of his beasts. I assume he looks nothing like his former self."

"Well, if I never see him again, I'd be happy." Aldrnari flicked a scrap of bread into the waters. Varn had started to teach him different spells to conjure food and drink. They did not turn out to be edible. "Can you make me another mug of water? The salt in the air from the sea always makes me thirsty."

Varn laughed. "Of course, lad. You'll need all the strength you can muster to have an audience with her parents." He pointed up to Mavelley, who perched joyfully in the crow's nest.

"Don't you think I'd do well enough with my charm?"

"If anyone could, it'd be you." Varn shook his head. "Now, watch my hands on this spell. It's quite simple." He slapped his palms together and swirled one above the other. "Dust in air and air around. Cause this dust to lift from ground."

Trails of dirt formed a mass between his hands. It quickly hardened into the shape of a cup.

Aldrnari mimicked Varn's words, but not a speck of energy trickled from his fingers.

"Maybe it's my hand movements," Aldrnari said. "I can never get it right."

"You should look at those books you were gifted from the elves. Katell led the Circle of Sorcerers for a short while." Varn returned to his post at the helm, looking across the vast waves the Tide's Requiem parted.

"I might be due for some reading," Aldrnari said to himself and headed for the lower cabins.

He thought of the strange book with blank pages. The dead tree on the cover seemed to be waiting for him to write in it. Yet every time he opened it, the poems he wanted to compose for Mavelley escaped his memory.

"The first one must be special," he repeated to himself.

Some of the other books he grabbed contained remarkable illustrations but were written in a language he couldn't discern. Trying to match the text with the pictures proved excessively difficult and made his head hurt. Reading the spell books made him want to write his own works all the more. It became a frustrating situation, and he ended up returning to speak with Mavelley.

Stumbling up to the sunlit deck caused him to shield his eyes. He must have been down longer than he thought. Time warped itself in strange ways whenever he opened the blank book. He'd noticed it becoming more frequent on the journey.

"Do you see anything out there?" he called up to Mavelley.

She descended the mast and grabbed his arm. "There's another ship out there, but I've never seen anything like it. Should I tell Varn?"

"Did it show any indication of being hostile? Like a black flag or red sails?"

"It's something else." Mavelley glanced back over the starboard side of the ship. "They flew a dark flag, but the sails resembled leather rather than fabric—like it was rotting."

Aldrnari turned pale. He took in a heavy breath that made his head spin.

"I know who it is," he managed to choke out. "Turn away. Tell our captain to turn. Now!"

Mavelley rushed to Varn while Aldrnari regained his senses. If spotted, there would be no escape. His former captain would summon a creature to pursue them without end. The Stormeye was about to cross their path.

He sprinted to Mavelley's side as one section of the ship rose from being jolted to the left. With the sudden movement, he toppled onto the fae and they rolled to the railing. His back crashed into solid wood, protecting Mavelley from hitting the edge.

"I'm sorry," he groaned and reached his arm over her to push himself up.

Instead, Mavelley pulled him closer. She pressed her lips into his.

"For luck," she whispered and kissed him again quickly.

His mind spun in a confusion of bliss, forgetting their pursuer.

Until Varn shouted at them. "What am I fleeing from?"

The ship leveled itself, and Mavelley relaxed her grip on Aldrnari's back.

"Why are we going so far off course?" Varn yelled again, looking like he was about to throw something at them.

"It's him," Aldrnari said, lifting himself with the railing's help. "Mavelley said she spied a ship with rotting sails. They're from the creatures he summons. It's Crowell."

"You had said he was near Northeal." Varn gritted his teeth. "Is he headed back there?"

"The ship was pointed toward it," Mavelley said as she fluttered to her feet. "My family told me he's trying to gain our powers."

"He's definitely going to spot us if we go to your forest."

"So it's bad if he sees us, right?" she asked Aldrnari.

"Yes." He rubbed his side where it hit the rail.

"Then we'll want to travel faster." She glanced behind them. "I think he's turning toward us."

"I'm not sure if I can outrun him for long," Varn said and tightened his hands on the wheel. "What he summons aids his speed."

A growing fear caused Aldrnari's mouth to go dry. If his former captain caught him, there would be no mercy given. He'd witnessed Crowell's rage on those who fled. It wouldn't be a quick death either.

He started to pace as he looked across the waves. He couldn't see the Stormeye anywhere. With any luck, Crowell hadn't seen the Tide's Requiem either.

"Where are your maps?" Aldrnari nearly jumped at his idea. "I know where he will never go."

Varn pointed to the stairs. "Top drawer next to the bed. You can't miss it."

"I'll plot a course to the northern lands. They're not far from here, and he's afraid to go to the port town. If I remember right, it's called Virfell."

Aldrnari ran down the stairs and threw open the door to Varn's room. As he said, the maps were rolled up in the drawer of his nightstand.

After unraveling a few of them, Aldrnari found the one he needed and headed back to the deck. He hoped Mavelley would understand their need for a detour. As much as he wanted to marry her, it would never happen if their ship entered Crowell's summoning range.

Mavelley kept watch from the crow's nest while Aldrnari gave directions for their course to the northern lands. Even before she informed them the Stormeye no longer followed them, Aldrnari could see a brighter glow in Mavelley's wings. With her being near the sails, traces of fae magic pushed them faster to their destination.

"There are the cliffs, lad," Varn said, pointing across the bow. "The port you mentioned will be our best stop. Many ships have searched the coast in vain for a better spot to dock."

"I guess my eyesight isn't as good as yours," Aldrnari said, trying to catch a glimpse of the shoreline. He motioned for Mavelley to come down. "I wish we'd made it to your forest. We could have had our ceremony by tomorrow."

"The warnings make it sound worse than it is for a fae to be married away from our forest." Mavelley grabbed his hand. "Most people do not see me because of my connection to it. If we were to wed anywhere else, I would be bound to this realm." She nudged him and winked. "Which isn't all bad."

"In some parts of the world, I could marry you two," Varn chimed in. "Human settlements often allow captains to perform the ceremony. Although, I'm not sure how you'd feel about an immortal doing it."

"You would make the perfect minister," Aldrnari joked and suddenly caught his breath from the captain's statement. "I mean, if we decide to go that route."

"I'm not sure we should try to reach my forest." Mavelley sighed. "Plus, I'll have to convince the fae to allow our union and not have you killed on the spot."

"Fair point," Varn said and straightened his hat. "I suppose if you two decide on it, there's no changing your mind. I've never led a wedding, but this is the first I've heard of a fae being in love with a human. And I've been around for a while."

"Let's reach port first before we decide anything." Aldrnari thought his heart might burst from his chest. He steadied himself against a rail and focused ahead. "I can see it in the distance."

13

It didn't take long for Aldrnari to stuff extra clothes in his bag of books after Varn ordered them to gather their belongings. A couple of guards met them at the gangway before they set foot off the ship.

"There's a fee for the security of your vessel, my good sir," the harbormaster said, stepping between his two brutes. "I can personally assure you nothing will happen to your ship while it is stationed here. No thieves or pirates are welcome in our land, and the penalty for any trying to sneak by us is harsh. I recommend finding another port if you practice those trades."

"We are travelers in need of supplies," Varn said. "Please excuse any rough appearance we may have. There were some unsavory folks on the seas. Is there a good place to rest?"

The harbormaster crossed his arms and eyed Varn carefully. "You have a strange resemblance to an old sailor who used to frequent these lands. It costs extra for information, but we can add it to your room and board."

He held out his hand, and Varn took out a few coins.

"Aye, this should do nicely," the harbormaster said in a more mellow tone. "You'll find our main tavern to be the best place for a room. It's not far from here. Stick to the main road and turn onto the side street past the blacksmith's shop. If you're looking for any repairs, I'd recommend stopping there. Sindrick can do wonders with anything he lays his hands on."

"Thank you. We will keep the place in mind." Varn motioned for the other two to follow. "We hope our stay brings light to your village."

He bowed to the harbormaster and led the way to the tavern. Aldrnari wanted to ask him more questions about Crowell but decided to hold his tongue. If Crowell was afraid of going to the northern lands, he likely did something to deserve a harsh treatment from the locals.

"Did you recognize the two guards with the harbormaster at all?" Mavelley asked Aldrnari as they walked through town. "They almost looked like you."

"I've never met them before, but we could be related." The thought made Aldrnari stop and look back to the harbor. "I always imagined my family was waiting for me at some strange port or out on the water trying to save me from Crowell. It would make sense that they are at the place I was forbidden to speak of. And the older I've become, the more I hoped none of them searched for the Stormeye. They wouldn't have survived."

"It's a good thing you're traveling with me," Varn said over his shoulder. "I won't let him do any harm. We immortals keep watch over our crew. It's a shame Crowell turned so far down the wrong path. He had a great enthusiasm for the outside world. I wish you'd met him before darkness corrupted his soul."

Aldrnari shrugged. He tried imaging Crowell having a similar temperament to Varn. It seemed more believable that Varn would turn evil than to have Crowell be anything other than a villain. If it came to it, he would escape another immortal to follow his fae.

"We must be getting close," Mavelley said. "I smell food."

She closed her eyes, and Aldrnari caught a whiff of fragrant meats cooking on an open fire.

For having no recollection of the town, a sense of familiarity filled him at the sight of the tavern. It reminded him of a childhood dream—like a place he visited in memories long forgotten.

"I've seen this place before," he whispered to himself. "How could I know about Virfell?"

Mavelley hugged his arm while they approached the entrance.

"Here we are," Varn said and opened the door for them. "If you need it, I can cover the cost of an extra room. I know you'd like to wait to share a bed until you are married. It's the least I can do for holding you both up for this long. I promise to get you back to the forest soon."

"It's not your fault," Mavelley said. "If we don't make it there, we can get married—"

"I'll strike you where you stand, villain!" the man behind the bar shouted and rushed toward them.

He brandished a sword as Aldrnari readied himself between the madman and Mavelley.

"Whoa!" The barkeep stopped like he had been struck and dropped his sword. "Apologies, strangers." He clasped his hands and bowed. "The tall one there reminded me of someone. Please pardon my advance. Your first round's on the house."

"I'm guessing my brother has been around these parts," Varn said, relaxing his defensive pose. "I can put your mind at ease. I bear no resemblance to his nature or vices. I've been seeking another one of my kin who went missing."

"Come in, and let's raise a glass to those yet to be found." The barkeep returned to his station and filled three wooden mugs. "The name's Jack if you'd like to get more acquainted."

"A pleasure to meet you, Jack. I am Varn and come from a secluded island. Two of my brothers ventured out before me."

"Forgive my assumption, but does one of your brothers command the Stormeye?"

"Aye, and he turned vile with his thirst for dark magic." Varn picked the cup up and took a drink before sitting down. "My other brother travels quite a lot. He doesn't look like us, often like a common beggar with a strange speech. Ben is his name."

"Sorry, friend. I haven't seen him around here." Jack leaned closer while Mavelley and Aldrnari joined them at the bar. "I usually know everything coming and going by these parts. That's why I was a bit on edge earlier. Someone reported the Stormeye within spy distance. He hasn't been this way in a long time."

"We had to outrun him," Aldrnari said and lifted the cup to his nose. "He won't come here. By the way, what sort of drink is this?"

"It's a family secret, but I'm sure you'll like it. I have a way of knowing these things."

Aldrnari took a sip. Sweet nectar blended with the cinnamon ale and made his tongue buzz with flavor.

"What do you reckon?" Jack asked.

"It's smooth, and I like the mixture. Is it a type of mead?"

"Partially." The barkeep placed his hands behind his head and leaned back. "To be honest, my daughters invented the drink. They're both around your age—twins and not married. I can introduce you to them if you like."

Aldrnari coughed from the remark, spitting some of the ale back into his cup. "I am quite happy with the one I found." He put his arm around Mavelley. "We would be married already if it wasn't for certain circumstances."

"Well, there's another reason to celebrate. Forget what I said earlier. I can sense you two are destined to be crossed. I have a knack for it."

"I'm sure you do," Mavelley said under her breath and laughed to herself.

"Does your land allow marriages by ship captains?" Aldrnari glanced back to Varn.

"Indeed it does." Jack grabbed an empty mug and pounded it on the wooden bar. "Listen up, everyone. We have a young couple ready to wed. Who would like to raise a toast to . . . I don't believe I caught your names."

Aldrnari cleared his throat. "The lovely lady here is Mavelley, and I go by Aldrnari."

Pain shot through his cheek where Jack slapped him without warning. He shook it off and grabbed the stool, holding it up toward the barkeep.

"Get out!" Jack exclaimed in wonderment. "Sorry, not like that. I mean, are you being serious?"

"Yes." Aldrnari cautiously lowered the stool.

"Were you taken by Crowell?"

Aldrnari nodded and rubbed his cheek. "Varn took me in after I escaped. I met Mavelley shortly after."

"After all these years." Jack ran a hand through his graying hair. "Hey, Sindrick," he called across the tavern. "You'll never guess who has returned."

"What's going on?" A man roughly the same age as Jack came up to the bar.

He fumbled with his hands like he was about to draw a weapon, but a terrifying look overcame him, and he turned pale.

"Take the salt from the sea!" The man gasped, pointing at Aldrnari. "He looks like a younger version."

"I didn't see it at first," Jack said. "Now that you point it out, he looks the spit of his dad. Sindrick, watch the bar. I'll tell him."

Jack spilled one of the bottles in his haste to run out of the building. Sindrick stepped behind the counter. Scars covered most of the man's face and arms. A simple stocking cap hid what Aldrnari assumed to be bald spots from whatever burned the man staring at him.

"Can someone tell me what is going on?" Aldrnari asked.

"You are here." The man smiled. "Your parents, Dan and Rena, have been praying for this moment since you were young." His expression turned grim again. "Crowell is not here too, is he?"

"No. He never comes near this place. That's why it's a safe port."

Sindrick let out a heavy sigh and rested his elbows on the bar. A worn set of bracers wrapped around the disfigured skin of his forearms. Uncut gems and symbols were embedded in the leather, some of which tattooed themselves further up his arm.

"It's a miracle you were able to escape Crowell's tyranny," he said, scratching the unkempt stubble on his face. "I've heard it's gotten worse. There's a song we sing for the children about him."

"I'd love to hear it," Mavelley said and let her wings glow. "You should hear some of the poems Aldrnari tells as well. They are delightful."

"Unfortunately, this one is not pleasant. It is more of a warning." Sindrick folded his hands together. He hummed a dirge before going into the words.

Of all the ships upon the sea, child,
There is one you must not venture near.
It hunts the creatures of the deep wild
Causing all other vessels to fear.
The captain drinks the sea creature's blood
And skins them alive to coat his hull.
Then, like the consuming of a flood,
The crew eats the rest until they're full.
Beware, my child, of the dead hide ship,
The abomination of the sea.
If you wander close, your mind will slip;
From its fleshy sails, you cannot flee.
The soulless ship that should never be.

14

Aldrnari closed his eyes to let the words of the melody reverberate inside his mind. They spoke too well of his life on the Stormeye.

"Thank you for sharing with us," Mavelley said. "It is sad but beautiful. My sisters told me of Crowell's ship. If we get back to our forest, I will recite that song to them."

"It was this boy's mother who composed it." Sindrick tapped the bar near Aldrnari. "We thought you'd never return. Crowell certainly hasn't since the day he fled. I think the beast shook him to his core."

"For as long as I was on the ship, he never set foot on land," Aldrnari said and took another sip of the mead. "He warned us all of a creature, waiting to attack him if he tried. I'm guessing it's the one from here. Does it harm any of the townspeople?"

"Not anymore. Jack killed it on the night—" Sindrick looked towards the entrance. "He and Dan should be back soon. You probably met your brothers already. They watch the docks."

"I have brothers too?" Aldrnari's cheeks felt warm. "How big is my family?"

"The people here have lots of kids. You've got two brothers and a few sisters. Rena might be having more. I don't often see her in the tavern."

Before Aldrnari could respond, the door swung open. Jack stepped inside with another man close behind.

"My son!" the man exclaimed. "I thought we lost you to those pirates." Dan rushed over and wrapped his arms around Aldrnari. "I'm so sorry I couldn't keep you safe. Your mother was about to have another child—your brother. We tried to find a way to bring you back, but there were many complications with the baby. All we could do was pray. And now, here you are. It's truly a miracle. How are you? Were you safe?"

"Crowell protected everyone on his crew," Aldrnari said, not wanting to admit how he was treated. "We finally were close enough to land, and I managed to sneak off the ship. Then I met

Varn, we went to a festival, and the greatest thing happened." He slipped away from his father and held Mavelley close. "I met Mavelley, and we are engaged to be married."

He noticed the strength in her wings had diminished significantly from when they first met. She used more of her leg muscles to stand, no longer able to float above the ground.

"I see," Dan said and eyed Mavelley with suspicion. "Why don't I have Jack get a room ready for her at the tavern. I have room for one other, and it wouldn't be wise for you two to be together before your vows."

"What about Varn?" Aldrnari glanced at the immortal who sat quietly near the edge of the bar. "I had planned to split a room with him. Mavelley would have her own."

"I shouldn't stay long," Varn said. "It looks like you two may have found the path you were searching for. I should get back to the elven lands."

"What? How are we supposed to get to the forest and get married?" Aldrnari's excitement turned to an uneasy pit inside his stomach.

"She saw it too," Varn said, motioning to Mavelley with his cup. "The storms are growing larger. And with pirates lurking nearby, you wouldn't make it in one piece."

"But I thought it had to be there."

"It will be better this way, my love," Mavelley said and gently squeezed his hand. "I will tell you more soon. I think your father wants to speak with you alone." She turned to Dan with a smile. "I'll check into a room. It's wonderful to meet you."

She motioned for Jack to follow her to the other end of the bar. Aldrnari wanted to ask her more, but his father grabbed his arm.

"I want you to know you are welcome to stay with us as long as you like," Dan said and glanced at the others watching them. He leaned in to whisper. "There's something about your companions. We should step outside."

Aldrnari followed his father into the street.

Once they were farther from the tavern, Dan motioned for him to get closer.

"I have a strange feeling about the girl in there," Dan said as Sindrick slipped outside to join them.

"What do you mean?" Aldrnari asked.

Dan crossed his arms and sighed before continuing. "Do you really know the captain you came with? He looks just like Crowell."

"That's what I thought too," Sindrick remarked. "But I think we can trust him. If Varn helped save the boy, he must have a good heart. What do you have against his fiancé?"

"It's a deceptive beauty. She's one of those spell casters. You know how I hate magic. It's the reason Aldrnari was taken in the first place." Dan held up his hand to show a missing finger and turned to his son. "I'd stay away from her if I were you. She can't be trusted. Jack has a couple of twins near your age. They're both lovely and unwed. I'm sure one of them would marry you."

Dan's harsh words bewildered Aldrnari. He clenched his fists, ready to fight his way back to Mavelley's side.

"You're too rash in your judgments," Sindrick said. "Believe me. I was hurt the most by spells and magic."

"You're no better than the rest of them with your enchanted oddities." Dan shook his head.

"I don't care what either of you says," Aldrnari said, sliding his foot back to balance his weight. "For years, I've been told what I am supposed to do and how I am supposed to think. Do you want to know the truth? Both of my captains were from the isle of immortals and are brothers. Varn supports my love for Mavelley enough that he was willing to take us back to her forest—the forest of the fae. She is not human but one of the creatures of light. Her magic is unbound by the restrictions of this realm, as is our love. So if either of you wants to stop our marriage, you'll have the might of immortals, fae, and an escaped pirate to match."

The two men standing before him stared with gaping jaws. Dan turned and marched away without another word.

"I knew she was more than human," Sindrick said, smiling wide. He looked toward Dan, who retreated down the dusty road. "Your father will come around in time. Most of the people in town like to stick with the old ways. I'm not like them. Whatever you need from me, just ask. In fact, you might want to stay at my shop. I've plenty of extra beds after the last apprentices left."

"Thank you." Aldrnari exhaled slowly and relaxed his hands. "I need to find my future wife and make sure she's okay. I didn't know there was so much hostility against magic users. I've tried learning some spells myself."

"You would make a great caster." Sindrick followed him back to the tavern. "If you'd like to try your hand at alchemy, I have a few tricks to teach you. That is, if you decide to stay in Virfell longer. It would be nice to apprentice a student who sees wonder in the mystic arts."

Aldrnari considered the blacksmith's offer while they walked. Seeing the delight in Mavelley's eyes when he entered the tavern convinced him of what needed to be done—they needed to marry without further delay. Hopefully, Varn would stay and perform the ceremony.

15

"My darling, there is nowhere else I'd rather be than by your side," Mavelley said as she gazed into Aldrnari's eyes. "It was always a risk for me to be bound to your realm every time I wandered from the forest. I can't think of a better reason than to be with you forever."

Aldrnari held her hand while Varn wrapped a strip of silk around them.

"By the laws of this land and as the captain of this vessel, I hereby announce this fae and this human as husband and wife." Varn tied the ends of fabric into a knot. "May your bond never be broken, and the strength of your friends and family keep it firm. Hip, hip!"

"Huzzah!" the few who gathered cried out.

Aldrnari was glad his family witnessed the ceremony. Their cheers faded into the background as Mavelley leaned forward.

Their lips met. The kiss sent pulses of energy down his spine like the waves of light when they met in her forest. This one seemed more real—more connected to her than he had ever been. They were bound together in the same realm for the first time, unhindered by the veil between their worlds.

"Nothing is separating us now, I just feel you," she whispered in his ear. "The wind and weight of your land is mine as well. My heart is your heart."

Aldrnari kissed her again while some of the attendees gathered around them. They all placed their arms around each other and sang in mismatched harmonies.

The couple couldn't help but laugh at the strange ritual of merriment.

"Love is a commitment you must embrace every day," Jack said as the musicians continued to play. "For however long you breathe, you must strive to sow in the garden of love for one another. If you falter, you will drift apart in a tide of darkness. Fight against the darkness. Hold fast to the light and let your choice be for each other's well-being. Love is a rare commodity. Few find it, and fewer can keep it."

Aldrnari listened intently to Jack's words. Although still in awe that Mavelley wanted to be with him, fae or not, he knew her love for him would outlast any fault of his own. And he would commit his life to fulfill her dreams.

"If you like, you may both stay at my tavern," Jack continued in a cheerful tone. "I'm sure you would like to be alone."

A few approvals and remarks came from the onlookers.

"What do you say, husband?" Mavelley raised his tied hand to her lips and kissed it gently. "Should we find rest at the tavern or spend more time with your family?"

Aldrnari caught a glimpse of his father, who kept his arms folded during the ceremony. Although his mother appeared to be pleased with the wedding, Dan held a blank expression.

"I feel like we should get out of town for a while," he turned to Varn. "Are you going back to the elves?"

"Aye, lad." Varn sighed. "As much as I'd like to say it would be a good destination, the hostility against humans is greater than you know. It would be best for you to stay here for a spell. I'll return once I find out if it is safe. With any luck, the council has listened to Jodoc."

"I know a place you can go," Sindrick said, leaning closer to them. "It's a home in the north, not too far from here. It was our

—my first shop." He turned away like he was listening to someone and then came back with a smile. "It's the perfect place for newlyweds. There's a town nearby, but it is far enough away to be secluded."

"How long would it take us to get there?" Aldrnari asked.

"A little more than a day, but the road is safe to travel at night. I can get a cart ready."

"Wonderful," Mavelley said, placing her hand on Aldrnari's cheek. "A cozy place to be together. There will be plenty of places to explore once things settle down around here."

"Oh, there are great places to see up there as well." Sindrick grabbed Aldrnari's shoulder and pulled him closer. "You don't want to stay long. The winter gets harsh. I'll join you on your voyage up there. I need to make sure it's ready for visitors."

"It sounds like this blacksmith will take care of you two," Varn said and handed Aldrnari one of the silver coins. "You might need this for your stay. Remember to use it wisely and give it away often."

The captain winked as Sindrick led the two off the ship and back into town. Aldrnari's eyes met Mavelley's again. Together, nothing would stop their love.

Plants grew around the abandoned building. It made the structure hard to see in the distance while traveling the path to Sindrick's old shop.

A familiar scent of sea mist filled the air the closer they came to the wooden door. Its tattered hinges did not have the welcoming allure Sindrick boasted of when they were back in Virfell. Aldrnari began to doubt it would be suitable for him and Mavelley.

"It has been longer than I remembered since I've been up here," Sindrick said and knocked on the door. "I'm certain it's unoccupied."

Aldrnari rubbed Mavelley's shoulders. She wore extra layers for the cold, but something else caused her to shake. Ever since their marriage, he noticed more of her glow fading, and her wings no longer remained transparent. They became a brownish hue, like leaves disconnected from their branches.

Sindrick knocked again and used his key on the lock. To their relief, it was not as worn as the rest of the rusted metal.

With a couple slams of his shoulder, the door loosened from the frame and swung open to reveal the sparsely furnished home. Chewed remnants of a stool next to piles of gathered fabric littered the large room. Fragments of rocks and precious gems remained untouched under a layer of dirt on an old workbench.

"I'm sure it's not as bad as it looks," Aldrnari said, noticing Mavelley's expression of worry. "You do have extra supplies, right?"

"Well, there's plenty of spare roof in here." Sindrick ran his hand across the scars on his arms. "I think I have some bedding in the back storage and enough rope to make you some shelves. It's an old trick I learned. It shouldn't take long for me to fix everything up for you. Why don't you take some food and have a picnic by the sea? It's a lovely view."

"How do we get there?" Aldrnari asked.

"Keep following the road to the west. You can't miss it." His eyes glazed over as he became lost in thought.

"Thank you again for your kindness." Mavelley placed a hand on his shoulder. "We won't be too late. I'm sure you can make it back to town before nightfall."

"Yes, nightfall." Sindrick picked up some of the gems on the table. "My enchantments held," he muttered. "The shadows crawl and roam, but they cannot tempt me again. The cliffs . . . the cliffs. Mind your footing near the cliffs."

"We will be careful," Aldrnari said.

Sindrick turned to him like he didn't understand what he was saying.

"You should help him clean up while I get our cart unloaded," Mavelley whispered and nudged Aldrnari forward.

"I can take care of everything here," Sindrick said quickly with a joyful expression. "This is my mess to sort out. You two enjoy yourselves. See the sights and fill your bellies. This is your day to celebrate."

Aldrnari grabbed Mavelley's hand as they returned to the cart and packed a small sack of food. While she was distracted, he slid the blank book from the elven kingdom into their bag. It would be the perfect time to write her a poem.

Something about the place sparked inspiration for the perfect one. He could hardly wait to write it while they strolled along the path to the sea. There was something about looking across it that brought a stillness to his soul.

16

"What do you think of it?" Aldrnari asked as they sat along a field of grass before it dropped into the sea.

"It's beyond what I imagined growing up." Mavelley leaned back and let the sun encompass her face. "Everything here is so real. Being stuck between the worlds never allowed me to experience one fully. I know they call it a curse, but I feel so free. Thank you for letting me share this life on your ground."

"I must confess that I would have liked to be bound to your realm, but I'm happy living wherever you are." Aldrnari smiled and placed his hand on the bag. "I have something I want to show you." He took out the book with the strange tree on the cover. "This is completely blank inside. I thought it would be perfect for filling with our dreams and poetry. There's one I've been formulating in my mind, and it's ready for the page."

"That sounds lovely. Please write it down for me." Mavelley huddled closer while Aldrnari readied his ink and quill.

"It's new, and I've been trying to come up with it since we met. It's about you."

Mavelley's cheeks turned red, and Aldrnari kissed them quickly.

His feathered pen blew softly in the breeze, lifting from the waters below. He could almost see the words forming themselves on the page. Each line and curve begged to be placed on the unmarked parchment.

"One fae holds more beauty than any realm could contain," Aldrnari spoke aloud before placing the tip to the page.

As soon as it hit, ink spilled out from the shaft of the quill. He pulled it back in frustration at the growing spot. Smoke trailed up while the stain bled through the book.

The black ink twisted together in spirals to form words. Aldrnari watched intently as his poem to Mavelley wrote itself. The more he thought of her, the more it described her in detail—her golden hair, her emerald and blue eyes, her skin that shone like a million stars, and the fading of her wings when she was cut off from her realm.

The mystical poem unfolded in smoke and foam across the page as he continued to read Mavelley's story. Although he did not write it physically, it was the poem he envisioned in his mind.

At last, it came to the end of the final stanza and glowed a violent crimson.

Screams erupted from Mavelley, causing him to turn to her. A fog of shadows seemed to grip her from the side of the cliff.

He reached out but was too late.

The area filled with a dark cloud, and she vanished from his sight.

"Mavelley?" he cried out to the void. "Where are you?"

As he stood, the smoke cleared, revealing an empty spot where she had been. The strange vapor from the sea gave no hint to her location. If she fell, he would have heard it. She simply disappeared.

"This can't be!" Aldrnari's eyes were wide with fear and worry. "We are meant to be together. I felt our souls connect. Please, hear me wherever you are. Without your love, I cannot live."

He fell to his knees and replayed the final moments in his mind. There had to be something he missed.

Mavelley had glowed the same red as the words in his poem before fading into the smoke. The air still smelled of burnt ink.

Aldrnari looked down to the book, once again white like the events never happened. He held it up, hoping somehow he could see the fae inside of it—nothing but a blank page.

All of his dreams seemed lost to the shadows with Mavelley. Somehow, the book trapped her inside of it. He should have left it in its prison. If the elves had it locked away, perhaps they could release her from it as well.

Aldrnari didn't care about the pain burning in his lungs as he raced down the hill. His chest felt as if it had been ripped open, and his heart pulled from its chamber. The moments he shared with his wife were too brief to be taken away so soon.

Aldrnari's words choked back from escaping as he burst into Sindrick's shop. The blacksmith stared at him, holding a box of organized supplies.

"Shadows covered her," Aldrnari gasped between heavy breaths. "I don't know how but she's gone—in here."

Aldrnari held the book out to Sindrick, who set his container on the ground.

"Did you see anyone else?" Sindrick asked as he took the book. "What is this?"

"When I started to write about Mavelley, the ink somehow trapped her into the pages. I don't know exactly what happened. There was so much darkness." Aldrnari held his head and slumped down the doorframe.

"It's like her amulet . . ." Sindrick grabbed Aldrnari's wrist and pulled him up. "Listen boy, this could be the key to it all. Where did you get this?"

"The queen of the elves had it." Aldrnari wiped his eyes, itching from the smoke.

"There is something hidden inside this book. I know because this holds the same mystery as the necklace she wore."

"Mavelley never wore a necklace. Who are you talking about?"

Sindrick gazed out the window. Almost like he was expecting the person he spoke of to walk past them.

"A poisonous lover," he whispered. "She's never left me. I suppose a remnant remains of anyone we love with reckless abandonment."

"Please, whatever it is, help me return to the elves. Katell will know more about the book." He took it back from Sindrick, who stared at his empty palms.

"Yes, yes. The elves are connected to other realms." He ran into the back room and returned with a large pile of fabric. "Your father made this for me. If we leave now, we should be able to reach their shores by tomorrow night."

"Is that a sail?"

"It is." Sindrick's eyes seemed to have a spark of joy. "I've never told anyone about it, but I have a ship. Here, along the cove. I'm sure it survived over the years. It was my greatest work and last thing I ever did for her."

Aldrnari tried to force a smile to match Sindrick's sudden happiness, but grief overtook him, and tears streaked down his face.

"We will find a way to bring her back," Sindrick said in a calmer tone. "You came back to us when we thought hope had passed long ago. Against the threat of curses and rejection, you married the one your heart loves. And she is a fae. Their magic is stronger than any enchantment I've seen. Your bond breaks the walls of the realms."

Aldrnari tucked the book carefully into his bag and focused his eyes up the path where Mavelley vanished. "Lead the way to your ship."

The two trudged silently back up to the cliff overlooking the sea. Its tide pulled the waves away from a cove, hidden from the obvious path. An unseen force created a dark aura around the mouth of a cave. Jagged rocks broke themselves around the entrance, causing Aldrnari to step carefully to enter.

As soon as they were inside, he found the chamber held a small lake that trickled into the sea. A large and quiet object rested in the middle of it, Sindrick's ship.

Although it appeared to be made from rock, it swayed gently on the water.

"It has remained untouched," Sindrick said more to himself.

"I've never traveled this far north," Aldrnari confessed. "I know most routes across the seas, but we should keep in uncharted areas to avoid the Stormeye. Do you know of any dangers if we take a northern route to the elves?"

Sindrick looked at Aldrnari like he wasn't sure who was speaking to him.

"Our passage will be safe," he said at last. "Don't worry. I won't let any harm come to you again. Cowardice made us lose you the first time."

"I trust you," Aldrnari said, trying to convince himself he could. "It shouldn't take us too long if we travel straight west through the night. Once we get closer, I'm sure I can find the way."

He finished tying up the sails as Sindrick took a long pole from the side of the ship and launched them toward the open waves. Its hull scraped along the ridge, creating a shrill noise.

Aldrnari leaned over the edge to inspect the damage. Instead of it hurting the frame, the vessel sliced through the rock. A gap remained and spilled out the cave's water behind them, giving them an extra push forward.

Wind instantly filled the sails and carried them in the direction of the elven kingdom. Aldrnari watched Sindrick maneuver the ship alone. Its size was impressive for being able to pilot without additional crew.

Soon the skies darkened as the sun gave off its last rays ahead of them. Aldrnari found himself unable to keep his eyes open. He rested on the sturdy rail and let the waves lull him to sleep.

17

"Aldrnari, wake up." Sindrick shook him violently from his dreams of being with Mavelley again. "I didn't see it coming. They're almost on top of us."

"What are you going on—"

Aldrnari froze as an arrow landed near them. The end broke off when it hit the deck of the hardened ship.

"Is it him?" Sindrick glanced over his shoulder. "I can't tell in the dark."

Fear shook Aldrnari's senses into full alert, and he stood to view the ship. "Crowell would never come this far north. What's he doing here?"

He peered at the vessel in the distance. Its black hull and sails appeared to be more weathered than the Stormeye.

"I need your help to go faster," Sindrick said. "You've been on more ships than I have. Please, help me."

"It's not him." Aldrnari let out his held breath and rushed over to the ropes holding the sails. "We need more wind."

He untied some of the excess fabric to catch more air, but the other ship had already extended oars to increase its speed.

"They're still gaining on us," Sindrick called as he ran back to hold the wheel. "If it's not the Stormeye, who would be attacking us unprovoked?"

"I don't know." Aldrnari looked up at the sails, trying to will them to move faster. "Come on. Please give us an extra push."

Another arrow flashed across the sky and cut apart a rope holding the mainsail. It furled aimlessly in the air.

"It's definitely not Crowell," Aldrnari shouted back to Sindrick. "He would have summoned a creature to stop us, not a bunch of arrows."

The blast from a cannon vibrated the waves around them and jolted the ship from an impact. A large rope twisted itself around the mast, wrapping up more of the sail. It tightened as Aldrnari followed the line back to the dark vessel. Within seconds, their pursuers had pulled up next to them.

"Let down your weapons, and you might survive," a deep voice commanded from their assailants.

Sindrick raised both hands to show his open palms. Aldrnari did the same and obeyed the voice. It was unlike any he had heard before.

"Do not move," the voice commanded again.

Sindrick's vessel shook again from the boards extending from the other ship. Dark figures nearly jumped across it to land in front of them.

As Aldrnari suspected, they were not human in the slightest. Before him stood a creature his former captain hunted to no avail —trolls.

"State the reason for your intrusion on our waters," the one who spoke before said through his enormous tusks.

Aldrnari couldn't keep from staring at their goat-like faces. Each one was a different shade of gray or black with ratty hair covering their body. Strands of bone and leather wrapped around them in primitive clothing. The largest one had a row of skulls around his waist.

"I ask again," it said louder. "Why are you up here?"

"We had to keep north to avoid pirates along our route," Aldrnari said. "We didn't know you protected these waters."

"So instead of being plundered, you have chosen death." The troll lifted his bearded chin and let out a peal of braying laughter.

The others jeered and stomped their hooves in approval.

"Wait." Sindrick waved his arms higher. "Please don't harm the boy."

"Oh, and what use is a human to us?" the giant troll asked and stalked closer to him. "Does a worm have any say if it gets stepped on?"

"He can draw you a map to my cave," Sindrick kept a stern composure. "It is full of gems with more value than what you're wearing." He pointed to the many rings on the troll's hand. "I also made this ship from the materials inside. You can see how it is unbreakable."

"This is intriguing." The troll stroked the sides of his beard. "Your mast did remain whole after our shot. We do not miss."

"Please, spare his life and take him with you. He is a great navigator."

Aldrnari wanted to protest but was quickly grabbed by two of the trolls. Their coarse hair felt like scales across his arms.

"If what you say is true, you will both show us," the troll said and motioned for the others to restrain Sindrick. "That is, if our chieftain allows this. Gostav will decide your fate."

More trolls emerged from the shadows as they shoved Aldrnari across the planks to their ship. Each creature on board watched the two men closely, waiting for an opportunity to slice them down. Their square pupils widened in intimidating stares.

A stench of despair mixed with the rotting fish scattered along the deck. The decomposed carcasses of smaller creatures decorated the outside walls of the main cabin. Several tusks jutted out from around the frame of the captain's door. Each one had a name etched upon it in honor of the one who fell.

"I will speak with him first before you enter," the large troll said and motioned for the ones holding Aldrnari to stand guard.

They released him and Sindrick, forming a line behind the two captives. Slowly, the head troll pushed the bone door open and disappeared into the darkness of the large room.

A dim light did little to aid what resided inside the cabin.

Aldrnari could make out piles of human skulls inside the chieftain's room. He gripped the bag around his shoulder. It gave him some comfort knowing that Mavelley would be near him if he died—although trapped within the book.

"Who has come into the presence of Gostav?" a voice bleated in deep tones.

The guards behind them stepped closer, pushing the two forward.

"I am a blacksmith," Sindrick said, walking farther in. "I'm certain my name is of no consequence. But this one here is Aldrnari. He is a navigator and skilled map maker."

A guttural cough came from within and echoed into a snide laugh.

"You may approach my mighty throne," the voice responded.

Through the haze of the dark room, a throne fashioned from bone protruded from the ground. It slanted upwards so those looking at it would have to strain their necks to meet the eyes of the one who sat on it.

Gostav's face was weathered more than the others, with a series of scars running horizontally down his cheeks. Between each mark was painted a yellow and red dot to resemble the eyes of the other trolls.

When Aldrnari and Sindrick moved closer, the tall creature stood from his throne. Great horns spiraled above his ears. The graying hair on his body had been burned off to accentuate his toned muscles.

"My crew tells me you know of a hidden treasure," Gostav said and revealed his jagged teeth. "Enlighten me, trifling pests. What makes you so certain I have not found it already?"

"The ship we sail on was in there," Aldrnari said. "I can show you exactly where it is."

"So the named one has a voice as well," the chieftain sneered. "I suppose you want us to spare your life in return for the knowledge."

Aldrnari looked over at Sindrick, who nodded.

"If we find this treasure, I might consider it," Gostav said. "I am curious. How could a runt like you know how to navigate these waters."

"I was in charge of the maps for many years under a captain known as Crowell."

The chieftain slammed his fist on the throne, breaking off a chunk of it. "The coward of the Stormeye. How dare you come into my presence? If he is following you, your life ends."

"He's not," Aldrnari said quickly. "We were in the northern seas to avoid him. I was his captive and escaped."

"You spit lies! No one could escape." Gostav bent down and glared at him. "That man slaughtered my people without remorse. Our island has been lost for many years."

Aldrnari's heart nearly stopped as he swallowed hard. "I speak the truth. Although I fear he may be hunting me as well."

Gostav let out his hacking laugh again.

"It's true." Aldrnari gripped his bag tighter. "Whatever happened to your people was not by his hand. I've been with him since I was young, and he never found trolls."

Silence fell upon the room as the chieftain's roars ceased. He looked again at Aldrnari in a way that made him feel like the troll was staring into his soul.

"The reports were true," Gostav said, returning to his throne. "My ex-advisor told me it was the storms. Nevertheless, if given the opportunity, I will take Crowell's head."

"Does this mean you'll let us go?" Sindrick asked.

"I give you my word. I'll let you go once we find the treasure. We share a mutual enemy, and I will repay him for summoning a creature to attack me before I learned of his power. The wreckage swallowed my mistress." The chieftain waved his hand for them to go. "Get your map ready. I need no more interruptions."

Those who had led them to the cabin stepped inside. Aldrnari complied with their nudging to avoid being grabbed again. The first troll they encountered returned inside and whispered to the chieftain.

Although his words were inaudible, Gostav's deep voice reverberated from the wood chamber. "Yes, I promised to set the blacksmith free, but the navigator I may keep. My last one almost ran us into a storm. We could reclaim the seas again."

The rest of his words became muffled by the other trolls jostling Aldrnari forward. Soon, the large one emerged from the cabin with a slight grin.

"Show us where this cave is," he said and shoved the guard next to Aldrnari. "You should be quick about it if you want to keep your head."

The troll brandished a crude dagger from his belt, causing the skulls to rattle together. Aldrnari took in a deep breath to calm his nerves. His whole life, he'd been threatened by pirates to do as commanded or be tossed overboard.

"Allow me to draw it out," he said and reached into his bag, tracing his fingers across the tree on the book's cover. "I have some paper to prepare. Is there a better place to work?"

"Is the deck of our ship not good enough for you?" The troll pointed the tip of his knife to Aldrnari's throat.

"This is fine. Let me get the ink ready." Aldrnari sat down and took out the book, opening up its empty pages. "Please forgive me, my love," he whispered as he thought of a poem to trap the goat-like crew.

He wrote of them being tied up before describing their fierce looks. If they somehow ended up near Mavelley, he wanted them bound and unable to attack.

"What are you writing?" the troll asked, looming over him.

Aldrnari penned the words faster, beginning to fear the book may have only worked the one time . . . until he wrote Gostav's name.

The ink once again drained from his quill. It flowed across the first page and sunk through to others. He flipped through the collection of poems about the trolls.

"Enough of this!" A hoof stomped next to him, knocking the rest of his ink bottle onto the book.

Smoke rose around it and boiled off the excess liquid. Trails of black snaked around the troll's legs, binding him where he stood. Shouts soon resounded from the rest of the crew before they passed into a mist.

"Run!" Aldrnari picked up the book and grabbed Sindrick's wrist.

They dashed across the boards to their ship as the black sails from the troll's mast turned to ash and smoke. In moments, all that remained of Gostav and his crew were the words in Aldrnari's book, slowly fading back into a blank page.

"Did Mavelley experience the same magic?" Sindrick asked, resting his hand on Aldrnari's shoulder.

"Yes," Aldrnari choked out, trying to catch his breath. "I didn't properly thank you for helping me. You saved my life back there. I overheard them wanting to keep me as a prisoner."

"I told you I'd keep you safe." Sindrick looked up to the mangled sails.

"Let's get this ship patched up and then find a way to set Mavelley free from whatever is holding her from our realm."

Aldrnari didn't wait for Sindrick's response as he set to work untying the ropes that held their sails. He no longer cared which route they took to reach the elven kingdom. If Crowell or anyone else got in his way, he would bind them in the strange book.

"We know you can see us," it spoke inside his mind. *"She will be set free and bring all of us with her."*

"I'm coming to save you," he vowed, trying to ignore the darkness increasing before the dawn. "The light brought us together, and I will follow it back to your side."

A gust of wind picked up behind them, propelling the ship faster through the waves. Aldrnari smiled for the first time since

Mavelley had been taken. He knew she could hear him as hope ignited in his chest.

18

"Let them in," Varn said as Aldrnari and Sindrick stood waiting outside the entrance to the elven kingdom.

Remembering the way through the woods came easy for Aldrnari, but trying to convince the guards of an urgent matter to see the queen became useless. He eventually asked if Varn had returned, and one of the elves became eager to find him.

"I'm surprised to see you back so soon," Varn continued as they were escorted through the circular hallways to the inner chambers. "If the concern in your eyes tells me anything, I'll not ask about Mavelley. When was the last time you slept?"

"It was interrupted." Aldrnari leaned closer to whisper. "The troll chieftain attacked us."

"Gostav?" Varn blurted out. He recomposed himself and spoke softly. "I'm surprised to see you in one piece."

"This book helped me." Aldrnari opened his bag enough to reveal the dark tree of its cover. "It also cursed me. Mavelley was pulled in when I wrote her a poem." He walked silently for a while and blinked back his tears. "The trolls took us, but I wasn't going to be a captive again. I wrote them into the book as well—bound, in case Mavelley was in the same place. Sindrick said it's a doorway to another world."

Varn wrung his wrists and opened his mouth a few times to reply but failed to find the right words.

"I need to ask Katell about it," Aldrnari continued. "It was one of the books I found in her study."

"My brother, Ben, spoke the truth," Varn said and sighed. "He's with the queen as we speak. I'd been searching for him, and now I find out he was following us. Ben always had a knack for perceiving more than any of us. I'm surprised he's communicating normally with Katell. He likes to speak in cryptic languages."

"You're speaking of the strange magician who speaks gibberish, right?" Sindrick interjected. "He showed up at my shop a few times. I sold him some items, but he liked learning how I combined different elements to bring out their true properties. He might have been an alchemist who worked with my father. At least I assumed as much. He's impossible to understand."

"If he knows so much, can he help us bring back Mavelley?" Aldrnari slowed his pace as they approached the doorway to the council room.

"He is a watchman, like me," Varn whispered. "Our realm is being knocked upon. I fear what may happen if the doors are unlocked."

The guards opened the chamber doors and motioned for them to enter. Unlike the commotion before, empty chairs filled the quiet room. Their footsteps echoed down the path to Katell's study.

"Queen Katell, we need your help," Varn called out when they entered the library.

She stepped out from around one of the shelves and smiled at them. Her happiness slowly faded from Aldrnari's worried look.

"Please forgive me," he said and kept his head bowed to approach her. "You warned me of the darker areas of this room, but I took the wrong book. It looked empty."

"What do you mean?" Katell asked, uncovering a hood from over her head. "Show it to me."

Aldrnari lifted the book from his bag. It appeared to be pulling light from the magical torches into its dark core. A sense of despair and loss filled him again as he revealed the blank pages.

"This book can somehow write people inside of it, like a prison or something." Aldrnari turned to Sindrick. "This blacksmith can see into things better than I can. He said she is in there but behind a barrier."

"How is this possible?" Katell asked more to herself. "Who is trapped inside?"

Aldrnari couldn't hold back his sadness anymore and sobbed. "My wife, Mavelley the fae."

"Let me see it," Katell said, snatching the book from his hands. "I created a spell many seasons ago to lock the evil inside. I don't know why it would pull someone else into it."

"The fae is not the only one he wrote about," Sindrick said and stepped toward them. "He also used it to stop the trolls from killing us. It was a clever move. Saved both of our lives."

Katell stared intently at the open pages. Her forehead wrinkled, and Aldrnari thought he witnessed her hair getting darker. The black aura surrounding the book seeped in through her eyes.

"I cannot see past the wall I created," she said.

"Can you tell me if she is alive, please? I need to know," Aldrnari begged.

"What did you do to trap her inside?"

"I wrote a poem for her. At first I thought it might be the ink, but the book gives me a strange feeling. I need to get her out of it."

Katell shut the cover and turned to Aldrnari with a steady gaze. "I fear the energy of those in this room will not allow me to unravel this spell. I need you to follow me. Alone."

"I vowed not to let the boy out of my sight again," Sindrick said and held out his hand.

"My magic will work better with less distraction." Katell handed him the book. "This might be an issue if it's in the room with us. Keep it close to you while we are away, and we will return soon."

Sindrick stepped between them, but Varn caught his arm.

"Stay right here and trust the queen." Varn pulled him back with ease. "I need to find Ben again, but do as she says. We are in her realm, and she will keep him safe."

"There's more to this book than they know," Sindrick muttered.

No one else but Aldrnari seemed to hear him as Katell started toward the entrance to the living quarters.

"Where are we going?" Aldrnari asked, catching up to her.

A welling of despair crept into him again when Katell turned to him with a worried look. She didn't speak while they quickened their pace. Aldrnari wanted to run back and grab the book. It felt wrong to leave it with Sindrick, but he desperately needed to set Mavelley free.

"We can perform a ritual to see the fae wherever she is hidden," Katell said, leading him to a circular room. "My mother kept watch over me using a scrying spell. I've used it before to gaze beyond the worlds."

"Please, tell me what to do," Aldrnari followed her into a ring of candles.

"Come closer and look in the reflection."

Katell pointed at a large mirror in the center of the room. Her dark robe cast long shadows that flickered from each candle set up in descending platforms around them. Their light became more volatile, lashing their fiery tongues in opposition to Aldrnari's presence.

"There is a darkness in you," Katell said as she approached him. "Loss makes the energy wary. Hold fast to hope. We will find her, but I fear what it may do to you if you don't trust the light."

Aldrnari clenched his jaw. "Whatever it takes, I will bring her back."

Katell nodded and placed her hand on his back. She whispered in a strange language, causing the torches along the wall to ignite. Each one precisely filled every darkened corner.

"Since this is your first time, it may take longer, but do not tarry," Katell said sternly. "You must find her before any creatures of shadow are allowed to enter our world. They are deceitful and will try to tempt you. Don't listen to them. Focus on the purpose of your journey. If you do this, the darkness cannot overtake you. All that matters is your love for your wife. The light is strong within her, and it will guide you."

Aldrnari closed his eyes as Katell chanted the scrying spell. The sorceress's words fell over him in a trance, and his head drew closer to the mirror. Although he feared he would soon crash into it, his eyes remained closed.

"Speak her name," Katell said to him.

"Mavelley." Her name sang from his lips, and he tumbled into a weightless state.

He could no longer keep his eyes closed and opened them to stop the spinning sensation.

As he did, he found himself in an immense field of charred ground. A soft glow shone down from the mirror above him. Shadows loomed around him in a black fog.

Katell's chants moved through his mind as he became aware of his surroundings.

"Focus on her light, find your love," they echoed.

He filled his mind with the feelings that brought him to Mavelley. The light guided him to her when no one else could see her. It brought them together in the forest and continued to strengthen their love for each other.

"Mavelley, where are you?" He closed his eyes in the void between realms.

In a rush of wind, he floated through the endless black and hovered near a strange glow. It was her's, but in a darker shade.

Her wings had completely fallen off, and her garments appeared singed from an unknown fire. The light of the fae remained in a dull aura around her, letting Aldrnari know she sustained her connection to their realm. It also kept the creatures of shadow from approaching her.

The formless shapes withdrew from Mavelley's presence as she walked through the empty field. Aldrnari could almost hear them crying out to her, but they were muffled in the vision.

The closer he moved toward her, the more a force resisted him. He watched as she touched some of the shadows near her. The creatures became more human-like. Some resembled other fae and flew toward the darker ones.

"I am here," he called out to her. "Keep fighting them."

Mavelley did not turn. Something blocked him from her view.

"I'll stay with you in the dark if I have to," he said more to himself. "Don't give up. I'll find a way to get to you. Even if I have to write myself into this realm."

A frigid sensation pricked his shoulder. It crept along Aldrnari's spine and made its way into his bones.

He turned to see the face of a shadowy creature staring back at him. Its features clouded together to form a feminine shape. Instead of the bright and hopeful eyes like Mavelley's, the woman drew light into her pitch-black sockets. Her lips curved into a grimace.

"Desires are fulfilled in my world," the shadow spoke in dual tones that fluctuated high and low. "You can have limitless power once you create the bridge. I know you will. An unbreakable bond ties you to our realm. Let us cross."

Aldrnari pushed himself away from the creature, closer to Mavelley. In her light, the shadows could not grab him. He stopped shivering from their cold embrace.

"Come back," a distant voice called to him.

He focused on Mavelley and his purpose to bring her back to their realm.

"Aldrnari, come back to the light," the voice became louder as he realized Katell was shouting at him from the other side.

He followed the sound to the place he entered. The light spilling from the mirror was almost blinding.

When he opened his eyes again, he was staring at his reflection.

19

Katell stood over Aldrnari, shaking him from the spell. A sharp pain in his shoulder caused him to wince from her fingernails that dug into it.

"I found her," Aldrnari gasped. "She was inside the dark fog. And there were fierce creatures of shadow. Mavelley brought some to the light."

"She has not been turned," Katell said as she helped Aldrnari stand. "I fear there may not be a way to bring her back safely. The creatures were trying to slip through the passage we opened. I've fought them before. They are the Nox."

Aldrnari noticed some of the candles were extinguished. Others burned lower on the wax to make up for the lost light. They reflected on Katell's hair, darkened by the spell.

"We should tell the others," Aldrnari said. "Maybe they can help us bring her back."

"Go rejoin your companions." Katell sighed. "I need to make the council aware of what happened during the spell. We have not been this close to the darkness in many years. And I won't allow the Nox to try and gain a foothold in my kingdom again."

She glanced around the room, then briskly led him into the hallway and back to her study.

Sindrick had moved to the table and was tapping his fingers across the dark book. Varn stood like a sentinel with his arms crossed, gazing across the room.

"I'll leave you here and meet with the council," Katell said, placing her hand on Aldrnari's shoulder. "Please be careful."

"Thank you for your kindness." Aldrnari could no longer wait to have the book back in his hands, and he slid it from under Sindrick's grasp.

"There is a great wonder in your crew," Katell said, pulling the hood over her hair. "If I can aid the light's purpose for it, I am grateful. To speak openly, I've been lured by the thought of being a watcher with the immortals. But my place is here. Be safe and beware the corruption."

Aldrnari flipped through the book's blank pages as Katell swiftly departed.

"She's alive," Aldrnari blurted out. "There's a realm consumed in darkness and shadows. Mavelley is fighting to keep her light. The darkness fears her."

"Were you able to see her without using the book?" Varn asked while rubbing his chin. "My brother warned me of those creatures of shadow."

The empty eyes of the strange woman in the darkness flashed in Aldrnari's mind. "Katell called them the Nox. She said they've been loose before."

"Aye, lad." Varn looked down the hall. "I should go with her to speak with the council. Ben can talk in circles sometimes, and many don't take his opinions seriously."

"Isn't Jodoc with them?" Aldrnari asked. "I'm sure he would know what to do."

"Sadly, our friend left before I returned from Virfell. He took the queen's parents home when the council decided they didn't want her human father staying."

"Before you go, can you help me get back to Mavelley?" Aldrnari held the book out to him. "I need to see her again."

"Another journey could break the walls between our realms. I've seen them thinning. Ben did too. That's why I left to find him."

"You're probably right." Aldrnari sighed and slumped against the table.

"We should seek the light's wisdom in this," Sindrick said and stood. "This is what you've all been suggesting, isn't it? I don't know much about magic myself, but I've witnessed it. Crowell revealed it to me many years ago before he took Aldrnari. If his dark spells have a counter, it is surely whatever light you speak of from the fae."

Aldrnari pondered Sindrick's words as Varn seemed lost in thought. The immortal eventually wandered toward the council chambers.

Aldrnari pulled out a chair to sit. Katell's scrying spell borrowed more energy than he expected. His shoulder burned where she pulled him from the realms and made his body ache.

He closed his eyes and imagined being with Mavelley, helping her turn the shadows as they fought their way out.

Aldrnari woke to the sound of voices down the corridors. He noticed Sindrick watching him from behind a row of books.

"We cannot give up on the elves so soon," Varn's voice echoed from the hallway. "As long as I'm around, they will not do anything rash."

"And I won't let them take your crown," Roparzh said while he entered the study with Katell and Varn close behind.

"Thank you," Katell said and turned to Aldrnari briefly before gazing at the floor. "I'm sorry," she whispered while Varn went over to comfort him. "The council will not allow me to do anything further to help rescue your wife. They blame humans for what happened last time. Their hatred rejects any rational thought."

"Ben suggested going back to the beginning." Varn placed his arm around Aldrnari. "Although I am not entirely sure what he meant by it. He said he needed to talk to his friend and walked right through the wall."

"He sometimes appears in our council chambers by doing that," Katell said with a slight grin.

"I wonder if he's found a way to step between the realms." Varn let go of Aldrnari and sat in a chair beside him. "It'd be nice to use a similar means to set Mavelley free."

Aldrnari took his hand off the book and discovered his fingers were sore from gripping it as he slept. "It is a bridge," he said more to himself. "When I was on the other side, I could see the mirror I entered from scrying. Maybe she can see the book."

Varn leaned forward, "What are you—"

"He's right!" Katell interrupted him and flipped open the book. "Write, poet. Write of your love for her. The light between you will create a passage through the shadows. She will know it's you as you knew it was her. Whatever the distance, it will guide her to you."

Aldrnari took out his quill and ink before she finished speaking. He could feel her words spoken in truth beyond his understanding. It filled him with peace and steadfast hope.

"Let your soul cry out to her," Katell continued as he filled his pen. "Write, and do not stop until she finds you."

Aldrnari nodded, and the tip of his quill hit the paper. The book tried to take the markings for itself, but he continued to write over it.

For beauty, there could never be
One to compare with Mavelley.
In speech, in sight, in her embrace,
My heart was rendered to her grace.
Captured not by a vain allure,
But by a love that does endure.
It won't consent to memory
Nor be content with apathy.
Our hope traverses the distance
And reaches out with confidence,
Until we will at last remain
To share our life in love's refrain.

The ink continued to slip out with each line. Aldrnari used it in a flourish of words and designs. He closed his eyes as he penned from his heart.

Smoke rising from the pages stung his nostrils, trying to pry him away from what he wrote. Yet in the vastness of his mind, he imagined her running toward the words. A new sensation buzzed around him while he described her struggle against the dark realm.

Without warning, the ink covering the page glowed like a fire lit it from behind. Aldrnari's words opened in pinpoints of light, casting a reflection of his poem onto the ceiling. Soon the entire room shone as if they were in sunlight.

The book shook so violently, it knocked him back from the table. Another wave of energy shot out, making everyone fall to the floor. Aldrnari had to cover his eyes and peer through his fingers to view the brilliant display.

A stream of light blasted upward from the page and turned the paper to flecks of gold, sparkling in the air. Through burning eyes, Aldrnari thought he saw a being reach out of the book.

His quill sprung from his grasp and landed in the outstretched hand. The feathers glowed with an intensity that created magical flames around them.

Another arm emerged from the book as the quill pulled the body upwards. A shower of sparks followed the figure who lifted out. Pages grew around her as they wrapped the form in an elegant dress.

Her hands dropped, and the dazzling light subsided. Markings of the poem covered her skin, but her smile made Aldrnari's concern fall away.

"Mavelley?" he gasped.

"Yes, my love," she said and stepped down from the table. "Your words shone across the wasteland." She held the quill out to him. "I believe this is yours."

Aldrnari took it quickly and wrapped his arms around his wife. Her body emanated a warmth from the light flickering off in tiny embers.

20

Aldrnari helped Mavelley ease into one of the scattered chairs.

"How are you?" he asked.

"Tired, but so glad to be out of there." She brushed her hair back, revealing more of the strange ink from his poem on her skin. "I've crossed between this world and the realm of fae, but the shadows . . . they were endless. It might have been a prison because I ran into some trolls who had been bound in a spell."

"It worked." Aldrnari had to laugh at the revelation.

Mavelley raised her eyebrow. "I'm guessing there's a story you need to tell me later, but there's a more pressing matter. We need to destroy the book. An entity kept telling me to merge with them. I think it was human once—a woman who called herself the

Orbivas. She said they were close to breaking through the veils, and I believe her. Something is causing rifts between the realms."

"We've seen it too," Varn said and wrapped his long arms around the couple. "It's good to have you back."

Aldrnari glanced over to the table. "We don't have to worry about the book anymore. It must have been destroyed when you came through."

He rubbed his hand along the charred stain where it once sat. A dark smudge stained his fingers. It took a few tries to wipe it off on his pant leg.

"Is there a way to remove the words on you?" he asked Mavelley.

She looked around to the others before squinting at him. "What do you mean?"

"The ink or tattoos, whatever they are." Aldrnari pointed to the marks on her arms.

Everyone else seemed to be as confused as Mavelley.

"I'm not certain what you see, but it might be a lingering effect of the scrying spell," Katell said and stepped toward him. "Do the words appear malicious?"

"Maybe." Aldrnari rubbed his eyes. "I thought they might have been from my poem, but I can't read them very well. They are different."

"Did you sense anything traveling with you?" Katell asked Mavelley.

"I don't think so," she said and looked at her hands. "The shadows fled from the light coming from the other side."

The same feeling Aldrnari had when the voice spoke to him trailed along the back of his neck. An evil presence clung to the words on Mavelley. It created a dark aura.

"We need more light," he said and reluctantly stepped back. "Is there a spell you could craft to get them off?"

"Yes." Katell stepped between them and held her hands out. "You should cover your eyes."

Aldrnari did as she requested and said a silent prayer for Mavelley.

"Spirits of the light, circle and delight," Katell chanted. "Bring forth your display. Ignite and play to banish the night."

Blinding flashes pulsed through the room. Aldrnari squeezed his eyelids closed and had to turn his head from the rays piercing his soul—expelling any darkness within him.

"It's done," Katell said and breathed heavily.

Aldrnari had to blink due to the remnants of her spell. When he finally focused on Mavelley, the stains from the words had vanished entirely.

"I did feel a presence leave me," Mavelley said and grasped Katell's hands. "Thank you."

Katell nodded with a weary smile. "Is everyone else okay? Where is Sindrick?"

Aldrnari looked down the rows of books but did not see the other human.

"He might have returned to his ship," Aldrnari said and returned to Mavelley's side. "You should see it. It survived an attack from Gostav, the troll chieftain, which is part of the story I need to tell you."

Katell cleared her throat. "You should all return to your ships. I need to inform the others what happened, and I doubt they will want you here."

"Please allow me to come along," Varn said. "You shouldn't have to go alone."

"As much as I wish for you to speak in my place, it is my duty." She folded her arms and gazed at the floor. "Go and be with your crew. I will send for you if it is safe to return."

"Whatever happens, I'll inform you either way," Roparzh said, stepping from his post by the entrance. "And she will not be alone when she speaks to them."

"Thank you," Katell said to him.

"You know, there's no one saying you have to tell them right away," Mavelley said and pulled herself up with Aldrnari's help. "I can sense you expended great energy to cast the spell. You should rest a while. It will also give us time to reach the dock."

Katell gave her a warm smile and held a hand out to Roparzh. He wrapped an arm around her carefully. Being attentive to her steps, he escorted the queen of the elves from the room.

In the same manner, Aldrnari took Mavelley's hand and helped her to the doorway.

"There are many questions I have about the other realm," Varn said, stepping in front of them to lead the way. "However, we should find Sindrick first."

"What will we do if he's not at his ship?" Aldrnari asked.

"That's part of my concern." Varn moved quickly through the corridors of the elven kingdom. "I sensed he had been swayed by the lure of darkness when we were in Virfell. The way he spoke of Crowell made me hope I was wrong in my assumptions. I should've stuck with my instincts and never left you two alone with him."

"I'm sure he's fine." Aldrnari didn't want to think ill of the man who helped him escape the trolls and free Mavelley. "Let's get back to the docks and wait to hear about Katell's meeting with the council. I also want to see if Jodoc left any of his books behind. He's quite keen on songs and poems. I bet he had some good ones tucked away somewhere."

"He took them with him to Northeal." Varn paused and reached into his overcoat, pulling out a small book of elvish verse. "You might enjoy this. It's something I picked up for him from Katell's study. He should've been back by now. I hope the storms didn't slow him down."

"Something else I noticed in the other world," Mavelley said and took the poetry from Varn's hand before Aldrnari could grab it. "A storm showed up while I was there, but it was unlike any in this realm. Almost like it was stealing the weather away instead of bringing it."

Varn opened his mouth as she strolled past him, taking the lead.

Aldrnari laughed and nudged the captain's arm. "Thanks for the book. I promise we'll return it when we get through it."

"Hey, wait up," Varn said, jogging back up to the front. "You can't say something like that and not give any more details."

Mavelley shrugged and continued her brisk pace. Aldrnari increased his walk to keep up with them. He couldn't hide his smile as the three started an unspoken race to the docks.

Once they safely reached the Tide's Requiem, Mavelley translated the elven poems for Aldrnari. Hearing her voice recite the well-crafted verse brought him complete bliss. Varn had left them to search for Sindrick on the other ship, and they could finally be alone.

Aldrnari could think of nothing but the love he had for Mavelley and the gentle rocking of the waves. A collection of ancient poetry made it perfect.

Aldrnari gazed across the sea and wondered if someday his works would be recited in other tongues. Ideas spun in his mind of rhymes he could compose from their travels. He vowed to find another blank book to write his poetry—one he would make sure did not belong to the shadows.

The familiar sound of footsteps across the deck shook him from his daydreams and alerted him of Varn's return.

"What is it, my friend?" he asked, noticing the worried look on Varn's face. "What happened?"

"I'd better let Roparzh tell you himself," Varn said, stepping out of the way to reveal the elven guard behind him.

"Our queen did not tell the council what happened," Roparzh said. "As we were approaching the Grandmage, we overheard reports of a human sneaking through the hidden passages of our kingdom. We suspected it was Sindrick, so I came to check his ship. Finding out he is not on it gave me more worry."

Mavelley flew onto the rail and pointed down a path leading to the docks. "Is that him? It looks like a human to me."

The others turned to see Sindrick running toward them.

"Where in blazes have you been?" Varn asked as he crossed the gangway.

"I thought I saw someone I recognized," Sindrick said and turned to Mavelley. "I'm so glad you've returned."

He gave her an awkward hug and secured a lump of fabric sticking out of his vest.

"You weren't sneaking around the council chambers, were you?" Roparzh placed a hand on his sword.

"Not that I'm aware of." Sindrick scratched behind his ear. "But I got lost and might have been near there. I recognized the path back to the docks after a while."

"Good." Roparzh let out a long breath and relaxed his hand back to his side. "I'll inform the queen and let you know her response."

The guard turned, and Aldrnari noticed a trail of smoke coming off his neck. Looking closer, it appeared to be a dark aura from a word tattooed on his skin—the same as those on Mavelley. He wanted to tell Roparzh about the marking, but the elf had already sprinted down the path.

Sindrick pulled Aldrnari's shoulder down suddenly and took out the parcel he'd been hiding. Unwrapping the fabric revealed the dark book. It had not been destroyed as they thought.

"How did you—" Aldrnari began, but Sindrick held up a hand to stop him.

"Look," he whispered. "Look at the book. What do you see?"

Aldrnari watched him flip through the charred pages.

"We need to destroy it," Mavelley said, grabbing one of the corners.

"Wait!" Sindrick ripped out a page. "Look. There's nothing there. It's empty."

"Of course it's empty," Aldrnari said and felt the blood rush from his head. "How can it be empty?"

He stared at the pages.

"Remember when I told you it held a mystery behind it?" Sindrick crumpled the page and let it fall to the deck. "It's gone."

"What are you saying?" Mavelley stepped back from the paper.

"He has the sight." Sindrick pointed to Aldrnari. "Tell me, what do you see when you look at your wife?"

"She's beautiful." The words he'd written about her before slipped from his mind. "I mean to say, she is the strongest and most radiant being I've ever seen. Her beauty glows from within."

Mavelley's cheeks reddened as she smiled.

"Do you see her glow?" Sindrick grabbed his sleeve. "Does she give off an aura of light?"

Aldrnari looked at her arms, illuminating the area. "Yes. Isn't that something you all see?"

He looked to Varn, who shook his head.

Mavelley giggled. "Is it like a firefly?"

"I guess so, but you're more dazzling." Aldrnari smirked.

"It's not a glow for me," Sindrick said and ripped out another page. "But I can see she is not of any element occurring in this realm. Such was this book."

Varn clenched his fists. "If it's empty, that would mean—"

"Roparzh!" Aldrnari blurted out. "He had a mark on his neck. It resembled the ones on you when you escaped." He rubbed Mavelley's arm. "Did they follow you out?"

"I don't know." Mavelley held a hand to her forehead. "It was such a blur. The shadows surrounded me for so long."

"We need to get back to the elves," Aldrnari said and took the book from Sindrick. "If whatever I saw is loose, we don't have much time."

21

"We shouldn't leave unarmed," Varn said and twisted one of the boards along the cabin wall.

Aldrnari had to step back as the captain slid out a long drawer across the deck.

Wooden patterns covered the box, requiring a particular combination to unlock. Varn moved each piece of the puzzle faster than anyone could memorize. Within seconds, the lid sprung open, and he rifled through the contents.

"These must be concealed unless necessary," he said and handed a strand of rope to Mavelley. "If the elves know we are carrying weapons into the inner sanctum, we will have added complications."

Mavelley swung the thin rope in circles. It appeared to have a deceptive weight to it, like it was laced with lead.

"Do this," Varn said, holding up a pair of bracers to Aldrnari.

He twisted a large gem adorning the center, and a collection of five throwing daggers stuck out from the bottom. After turning the catch back to hide the daggers, he helped secure them on Aldrnari's wrist.

Varn went back to his weapon crate and grabbed two long canes. He handed one to Sindrick.

"We can use these," he said and pulled the top section to reveal a glint of metal. "They hide a long dagger."

"I am always prepared," Sindrick handed the cane back and rocked on the side of his boot.

A chunk of it broke off in the perfect shape of a carving knife. He did the same with the other side and held the two blades up with a smile.

"Of course, a blacksmith would be ready." Varn laughed and secured the cover back on his box of weapons.

"I'll bring this too," Aldrnari said and wrapped the book up in a piece of fabric. "Katell should know it wasn't destroyed. With any luck, she'll be able to lock the darkness into it again. We better hurry. Roparzh might have already found her."

Varn nodded and motioned for Aldrnari to lead the way. The four of them raced back toward the elven fortress.

It took them less time to reach Katell's study as none of the elven patrols were at their stations. A chill caused Aldrnari to slow his steps. The hallways had a faint aura of darkness streaking through them.

Mavelley pulled back his arm to stop him from entering the room.

"What is it, my love?" Aldrnari whispered.

"Something else is inside." She leaned around him to get a better look. "I saw a shadow, but not from this realm. It was like the ones surrounding me on the other side."

Aldrnari crept closer, with the others peering over his shoulders. He couldn't determine where she had been looking and grabbed the gem on his bracer, ready to unlock the daggers.

"Where is she—" Aldrnari was cut off by a sudden crack of wood and a brilliant flash of light.

"You cannot be here!" Katell shouted. "Flee this realm."

Another pulse of light radiated from the room.

As the afterimage from her spell faded, Aldrnari could see Katell in the middle of the study with her back to them. Roparzh held up his arm next to her, covering his face. The strange darkness in the hallways subsided from the entrance.

"Is it gone?" Roparzh asked, lowering his hands carefully.

Katell glanced behind her and locked eyes with Aldrnari. "You've returned. Thank the light."

"There's something we need to show you," he said and took a deep breath before unwrapping the book. "Whatever had been trapped in here might be loose."

"It is as I feared." Katell's skin looked paler than before.

"The words on Mavelley transferred to others. One of them landed on Roparzh."

The guard's eyes went wide, and he searched over his exposed skin.

"It's not where you can see it," Aldrnari continued. "I'm not sure anyone else can, to be honest. It's on the back of your neck."

Roparzh scratched behind his head and inspected his fingers. "I shouldn't be here. I've doomed us all."

"No, we can stop them." Mavelley rushed to his side and put her hands out to calm him. "It's hard to explain what I experienced on the other side, but I know one thing—the darkness cannot prevail over the light. Whatever is merging our worlds would have happened regardless of our decisions. The barriers have been weakening to a breaking point. Now, they are shattering."

"This is not the first time," Katell said quietly. "If the beings are loose in our kingdom, there is no hope for the elves. We will soon be against an army of our own people."

"Are they able to possess us?" Aldrnari ran his fingers through his hair. "What of the fae? Can they help?"

"The Nox will try to take our minds, but I have a feeling they'll meet resistance." Katell smiled and took the book from Aldrnari. "I never told you, others were freed from that realm. Two humans were trapped inside, and I helped them pull free. With Mavelley breaking out, the Nox wouldn't try tempting her again. And I see a light growing in you, young poet. Remain in it, and you will be shielded from the darkness."

Katell sat on the ground with her legs crossed. Everyone except for Sindrick joined her. He continued to pace near the entrance.

"Come sit with us," Aldrnari said to him, unnerved by the look in his eyes.

Sindrick rubbed his temples. "She's not here," he mumbled. "She can't be here. It's in my head."

"There's no one other than us in this room." Aldrnari stood to meet him. "You said it yourself, I have a gift. If I can't see anyone else, it must be safe."

"You're right. It's madness."

A faint scream came from down the hall.

"It's too late," Katell said and closed the book quickly.

Sindrick darted in the direction of the noise before anyone could respond.

"Where does that passage lead?" Mavelley asked, untying the rope from around her belt.

"The grand ballroom," Roparzh answered and unsheathed his sword. "I can feel a presence luring me there. It burns at the base of my skull."

Katell held up her staff to illuminate the area around them. "Trust nothing you hear from the shadows. The Nox speak lies and will do anything to deceive you. Lead the way, old friend."

Roparzh stalked through the hallways with the rest of the crew close behind.

Aldrnari loosened one of the daggers from his bracer when their guide slowed his pace. A rush of doubt wanted him to run back to the ship with Mavelley. His metal blade would be useless against a magical being, especially the Nox.

Something sinister waited at the edge of the walls, anticipating their arrival.

He swallowed hard and took Mavelley's hand, hoping his fear hadn't spread to her. She squeezed gently and took deep breaths.

"You don't have to face the darkness alone," he whispered. "We can defeat them."

Her posture straightened with confidence, and she nodded.

Katell turned with a finger to her lips. She tilted her head to the door in front of them. Without having to speak, the rest of the crew took their battle stances.

As she pushed it open, a figure blocked their way. Sindrick stood like a statue, wrapping his arms around himself.

Aldrnari approached him first and tightened his grip on the throwing dagger between his fingers. "Sindrick, why did you run from us?"

Sindrick slid his hands down. He slowly turned to Aldrnari.

"She's there," he muttered and pointed to a cloud of shadows on the far wall. "We cannot stop her."

Aldrnari stepped around him to get a better view of the chaos filling the room. Rows of elven soldiers held their swords against the nightmarish foe. Within the darkness, shapes appeared of the creatures seen from the other realm.

A humanoid shape floated above the rest, and her eyes met Aldrnari's. It was her—the Orbivas of the Nox.

"Eleanor!" Sindrick called out to her.

The woman turned to him and sneered.

"Silence, you old fool." Varn placed his cane in front of Sindrick. "We need time to prepare the proper spell."

Some of the guards managed to get near the shadow of Eleanor, but a rush of wind pushed them away. They fell back in line with the rest of the elves.

"There they are," Katell said and waved toward a group of robed warriors who were positioned at the center. "We need to get closer to the other sorcerers. They can help us."

Katell moved past Sindrick, but he caught her arm. "No. Stay back. It's my fault she's here . . . my curse. She never left me. I must go alone to stop her."

"Enough of these dark thoughts," Mavelley said and flicked the ends of her fingers.

A flash of light erupted from them, and Sindrick stumbled back, releasing Katell.

"We fight together." Mavelley nudged the elven queen to lead the charge.

Katell crouched and advanced carefully to the Circle of Sorcerers. Roparzh kept at her side with the others at their heels.

"What's happening?" Katell asked the first robed elf she came to. "Why isn't our side attacking?"

"We were waiting for you," the elf said and pulled down his hood.

His eyes smoldered in a dark aura, matching the blackness of his hair. He extended his hand toward them, and inky tendrils weaved through the air.

22

Katell slammed her staff on the ground, and it produced a blinding light.

"My eyes!" the corrupted sorcerer cried out. "Snuff them out."

The rows of elves turned their swords to the crew. Each one held an arm over their face to cover the effects of Katell's staff.

"Fall back," she said and lifted it above her while the crew retreated.

Roparzh stood between her and the shadows until they were a safe distance from the turned elves.

"Dim the light," he said abruptly. "Someone's trying to break loose."

It was impossible to distinguish anything other than the dark elves and the woman who had descended. To their surprise, she stepped closer, unabated by the spell.

"For years, I have studied this foe," Katell said, turning to her. "I will not lessen my defense nor see the elves fall again."

Roparzh snatched the staff from his queen and smashed the glowing end into pieces on the floor.

"Look!" He shouted and pointed to one of the turned elves at the end of the row.

With softer eyes, the petite elf didn't resemble any of the other guards. She looked older and kinder.

"It can't be," Katell gasped. "Dahna?"

"You see her too?" Roparzh gave a wide smile. "My mother has returned."

He reached out to her, but Katell wrapped her arms around his waist.

"Don't go," she pleaded with him as the dark words on his neck spread into his veins. "It's not her. She lived a good life for both of us. You must know in your heart it is a lie."

"She might have raised you, but you are not of her blood." Roparzh struggled to break free. "Your human side deceives you. I need to be with her."

Both were flung to the ground as Sindrick pushed them aside. "Eleanor, I won't let you do this."

"Join me, my love," her voice echoed through the room. "You helped me become what I am. Let me give you the power you've seen in me."

Sindrick clenched his fists and rushed forward. Right before reaching her, he stopped. Her gaze seemed to hypnotize his movements.

The man's body levitated as shadowy strings encircled his legs. A dark cocoon engulfed him, and another shape started to form beside Eleanor.

Sindrick's features appeared on the new creature. It clutched her feet and glared at the onlookers.

"You have already desired to become one with the Nox," Eleanor said to Roparzh.

The trails of smoke coming from his neck pulled him from Katell's arms and into the dark cloud.

He managed to fight his way out enough for the others to witness the change. In a cry of terror, his skin turned an ashen white as his eyes darkened. He clenched his chest before falling backward into the abyss.

"Do not try to stop us," Eleanor said and hovered closer. "Together, we will bring all the realms—"

She screamed as a blade pierced her shoulder.

The sound turned to laughter, and she removed the throwing dagger Aldrnari had let fly. Instead of blood, smoke spewed from the cut. It healed the area in seconds.

Aldrnari turned to Katell. "Can't you cast another spell?"

"This magic doesn't work so easily," Varn responded and reached into his coat. "Hold on to me and get down."

Aldrnari hugged Mavelley, bracing himself for whatever horror the Nox had for them if Varn's idea failed.

They huddled close to Varn as he gathered the fragments of Katell's staff and performed a quick summoning spell for a clay vessel. As soon as he lifted the glob of shards, Katell chanted.

Light sprang from the ground and formed a dome. Mavelley joined in, enhancing the magic that encompassed them.

"Keep going," Aldrnari said, unable to mimic the strange syllables.

Shrieks from outside their protective shell gave him a renewed vigor.

"You fools!" Eleanor yelled. "Simple tricks do not hinder my power. The Nox will take this world."

Aldrnari peered through the bright spell as the leader of the shadows stalked closer to them. But something else caught his eye and made him turn around. A new energy was pulling their magical net toward the door they entered.

The force did not weaken their protective shell. It made the walls more robust and increased their size.

A booming voice repeated the enchantment near the entrance. In a shower of sparks, a hole formed in their bubble, giving way to a hand that reached through.

Aldrnari released Mavelley and readied another dagger to fight back the intruder.

The opening enlarged enough for him to see a tunnel of light similar to the shell around them. A familiar face stuck his head through the gap—the beggar he met in Northeal . . . Ben.

"Brother," Ben said while the words from the enchantment continued to echo. "Bring your crew with me. They are here."

Varn turned to Ben and smiled. He nodded toward the others to follow his brother through the path of light.

"Quickly," Ben said and mumbled something else in a different language.

"Where are we going?" Aldrnari asked.

"Back to the docks," Varn replied. "Ben said his friends are there. We need to hurry."

Varn let the others pass into the long hallway of light and whispered something to the fragments in his hand. He threw the object behind him, creating a burst of radiant energy. It pushed back any looming shadows following them.

"What of Sindrick and Roparzh?" Mavelley asked from the front of the group. "We shouldn't abandon them."

"They may return to us," Katell said, moving past her. "The Nox never took my mind when I—" She stopped. "I didn't know a human could turn. Sindrick must have been connected to Eleanor in the past. He allowed himself to be changed."

Ben took her hand and led her forward.

"Come, greatest sorceress," he spoke like he chose each word carefully. "Your knowledge will save us all."

"What do you mean?" she asked.

He focused on the hallway ahead and chanted again to keep his spell from faltering.

Trails of smoke gathered together near the ceiling as the crew sprinted to reach the docks in time. Around them, cracks spread across the barrier. A large chunk of the hallway collapsed beside Aldrnari as he raced to keep up with the others.

A strange laugh spilled in from the weakened sides.

Aldrnari covered his ears to block out the noise, but Gostav's cackling continued to ring. The others were likely too far ahead to hear it, and they wouldn't recognize the bleating tone. The troll had to be right behind him as darkness became more prevalent than the web of light.

Each step became more challenging than the next. Whatever magic the others used to keep them pressing forward escaped Aldrnari, or he was too far away for it to have any effect. He had to rely on his own strength.

An oppressive feeling of guilt burned in his chest. He caused all of this to happen. If he hadn't taken the book from Katell's study, the Nox wouldn't be loose. Mavelley would never have gotten trapped in their realm to begin with. He had created the darkness closing around him.

Tears streaked down his cheeks as he fought against the desire to give up.

Something fell in front of him, nearly knocking him over—a rope. Mavelley's cord retracted and lashed out again. This time it wrapped around his arm.

"Hold on!" she cried out and flew ahead of him.

Aldrnari was swept off his feet as she pulled him toward the light. Sliding across the rock, he watched her wings glimmer again. The weight of his doubt left him, and he embraced the sensation of hope filling his heart.

"They're here," Mavelley said.

He stood outside the tunnel and found a vast army hovering near the docks. The fae had arrived.

23

"Quickly, lock in the spell," Varn said to Katell, who was leaning against him for support. "We will help you complete it."

Katell knelt in front of the tunnel. "I don't know how. This is something different. The one who locked them in before created a framework for me to follow from the book."

Aldrnari followed her gaze to the place Mavelley had snatched him from the shadows. The trails of smoke continued to grow and break down more of the light.

"Maybe you don't have to send them back," he said and focused on his ability to see between the realms. "They cannot cross the barrier you and Ben created to protect us. What if you created a larger shell?"

Katell tightened her robe and held out her hand, which Aldrnari grabbed to help her stand. She nodded to him with a slight glimmer in her eyes.

"Their influence stops here," she said and held up her arms. "Weave and do not break. Stretch around this darkened stain. Encompass those the shadows take as within this sphere they are contained."

Streaks of bright amber spun from her fingertips. The color reflected in her eyes as it glowed into a dome and pierced the trees.

The light intensified with the multitudes of fae ascending to assist Katell's spell. Each one held out their hands to keep it sustained. In a flash bursting toward the heavens, the massive barrier stabilized.

Aldrnari no longer felt the presence of the Nox reaching out to him. He let out a sigh of relief.

"My love." Mavelley squeezed his arm gently to turn him around. "We should tell them of our marriage. I know we had meant to before all of this."

His heart raced, and he let his jaw drop to speak. The words didn't come out.

"Don't worry," she said and pulled him closer. "I'll do the talking."

Mavelley led Aldrnari to one of the fae he recognized. It was the same one Ben secretly met in the forest. His mirrored armor reflected the golden tint coming off the spell.

"I'm sure you've received news of our wedding," Mavelley said and bowed. "I understood the risk of binding myself to this realm."

The guard held a hand out to them before they could get any closer. "I see the change. The queen has decreed you are no longer welcome in the forest. It caused a disruption when your husband first entered, and she fears a second occurrence if you were to return."

Mavelley looked to the ground and sighed. "I was afraid of her response. Did you try telling her what I told you when I first met Aldrnari?"

"Unfortunately, I never had the chance," the older fae said and crossed his arms. "Once I found out you had entered into the realm of the Nox, there was no way for me to approach her without an argument. I'm glad you're safe."

"Thank you." She smiled. "Aldrnari was the one who helped me find my way back."

Aldrnari's cheeks grew warm. "I'm not sure how I did it, but our love created a passage between the worlds. The shadows weren't supposed to cross over with her." He bit his lip, and a tear streaked down his face. "I feel like this has all been my fault."

"The gateways between our worlds have been opening long before your time," the old fae said and gently placed a hand on Aldrnari's shoulder. "You cannot blame yourself for events past. No one has enough power to rewrite the course of history. We must follow in its flow and try to steer our souls to the light. Do not trouble yourself over the queen's decree. She will allow you to return with time's passing. I'll make sure of it."

"Thank you, grandfather," Mavelley said and gave him a quick hug. "I don't know where we'll go after this, but wherever Aldrnari goes is my home."

Her grandfather turned to a group of fae gathering near the water's edge. "You would do well to keep company with the immortal. For being tempted in the same ways as their brother, Ben and Varn have held to the right path. I believe one of their companions has returned."

Aldrnari wiped his eyes and peered out to the area the fae had pointed out. A small vessel eased itself up to the dock. With the help of those on land, Jodoc secured its ropes and stepped across the gangway.

"Not all the elves have been lost to the darkness," Mavelley's grandfather said and hugged her again. "Go and be with your crew. I'm sure he will enjoy a friendly face."

Jodoc had a worried look when Varn reached him before the other two and whispered something to him. Aldrnari slowed his pace as their newly returned friend covered his mouth.

"There were trails of light overhead on my trip back here," Jodoc said and shook his head. "I knew it had to be the fae, but this is worse than I thought."

"Take your courage back." Varn tapped his cane sword on the wooden dock. "With the help of the fae, I'm certain Katell will find a way to restore the elven kingdom."

"It wouldn't be the first time," Ben said, who seemed to appear beside them. "In the darkest times, a small light will shine brighter. You're a watcher. You should know before you see."

A shout erupted from the edge of the dome before Jodoc could respond. They turned to see Katell waving at them. She pointed to a dark spot on the barrier.

Varn stayed behind to help Jodoc find his footing after being on the sea while Aldrnari raced ahead of the others.

"What is it?" he asked, trying to catch his breath.

"I'm not certain, but it looks like it's pressing against the spell." Katell looked around to the fae who were working to keep the light shining on the wall. "It doesn't seem to be hindered by the multitude of protections. How can it be possible?"

Mavelley leaned closer to the object. "It's moving."

"Someone is trying to push through," Aldrnari said and watched the shadowy hand create an impression in the wall. "Everyone, get back."

Beams of light shot out of the area once darkened by a hand. The amber shell melted away from the fingertips of the one reaching through.

"Keep it locked in!" one of the fae yelled beside them.

Aldrnari unhooked another throwing dagger, ready to stab whatever was breaking free.

A strange glow came off the hand. It had the darkened veins of the Nox at first, but changed to the flesh tone of an elf as more of its skin stuck through the energy field.

"Roparzh?" Katell rushed up to get a better look. "It is him. Help me."

She took his hand and pulled. Aldrnari grabbed above the elbow while the guard's arm continued to emerge.

The rest of the crew arrived as Roparzh stepped out of the barrier, looking as if the Nox had never changed him.

"I ran to the light," he said between breaths.

Katell helped him kneel while he reached toward the ground.

"They took control of my mind and body, but didn't remove my memories," he continued. "I remembered when you pushed them back the first time and rescued those two humans. I figured there was a chance your spell would free me." He rubbed the hand they had pulled out first. "It burned to be close to the wall, but I had to try. Thank you for saving me. I wouldn't have been able to endure it on my own."

Katell sat with him and held him close. "You have been closer than a brother my whole life. Thank you for returning to me."

"Wait a minute," Mavelley said and looked down the row of fae along the dome. "There might be others trying to get free. Did you tell the other elves about the light?"

"My thoughts were swarming with those of the Nox," Roparzh said and leaned back on his heels. "It's hard to say what was shared with the others."

"We should help them," Jodoc said and bowed to Katell. "That is, if you desire me to stay. The council decreed my exile with your parents. I came back to find Varn and followed the fae."

Katell seemed to be pondering his words and stood up slowly. "After my husband passed from this realm, I was treated worse than if I was in exile. It will not surprise me if the council remains in the darkness. I cannot choose for you to stay and help them or leave . . . as I know I must. My time for ruling has ended. I wish to be absolved as queen and find others more welcoming to outsiders."

"You would abandon them?" Jodoc asked and cleared his throat. "I didn't mean to be cruel. Sorry, your highness."

"They will not be abandoned." Katell motioned to the fae army and smiled. "The fae will find a way to free those willing to return to the light and establish the right elven leaders. In my heart, I pray you will be one of them."

"Where will you go?" Roparzh asked, regaining his strength to push himself up.

"Well, that depends on him," Katell said and approached Varn. "What do you say, captain? Ready to have a half-elf sorceress join your crew?"

"It would be an honor." Varn quickly bowed. "Since you're promoting Jodoc away from me, I'll need the keen senses of your magic. However, they may need extra hands around here and a sturdy ship. The Tide's Requiem would be the fastest one to take any recovered elves to a safe harbor."

Ben rushed up to them, speaking in different languages so fast that Varn had to tell him to slow down.

"I see your point," Varn said after Ben took a breath. He turned to Aldrnari. "The vessel you arrived on with Sindrick, how confident are you in being its new captain?"

Aldrnari struggled to get the right words out as his thoughts teemed with the anticipation of commanding a ship. "I would love to captain my own vessel—especially Sindrick's. Whatever it's made out of survived an attack from the trolls without a dent. It looked like it was meant to be piloted by only one person as well."

"It's settled." Varn turned back to Katell. "We'll go wherever captain Aldrnari leads. Ben said he would stay with Jodoc to help anyone reaching out from the spell."

"I'm coming too," Roparzh interjected. "I promised to protect her and will continue to do so, no matter the cost."

Varn nodded. "I'll gather a few personal items from the Tide's Requiem and meet you all on Aldrnari's ship. By the way, what do you want to call it?"

"There's already a name written on the side," Mavelley said as she peered toward it. "The Salty Eleanor."

24

Aldrnari looked over the woods that once held the great elven kingdom. The magical shell glistened in the sunlight as darkness continued to fill it. Outside the dome, the fae worked to keep the spell secure and patrolled for any reaching out to the light. Some had already stepped out to be greeted by the welcoming company. It gave the new captain peace while his ship slid further into the open sea.

He knew the builder of The Salty Eleanor would never return. Sindrick seemed to be drawn to the Nox before they emerged from the book. Once he faced the leader of the shadows, his fate was drawn to her. And with her, he would remain—beyond the amber walls.

When they reached Virfell, Aldrnari hoped to tell of Sindrick's sacrifice and his aid in saving Mavelley.

"The shipwright was quite the crafter," Varn said beside him. "I used to think the strongest ships were only fashioned on our isle—this one is beyond anything I've seen."

Aldrnari nodded and continued to keep the wheel steady. "It's a wonder how easy it is to pilot. I didn't have much practice before. But from watching others at the helm, I imagined this one would be challenging."

"You're a natural helmsman. Sometimes the captain chooses their ship, and sometimes the ship chooses its captain. I feel you were drawn to each other."

"I get that a lot." Aldrnari smiled and looked up to Mavelley.

She leaned out from the crow's nest like it had been her home. Her delicate wings fluttered in the gentle breeze with the sails. For growing up in a forest, the fae appeared to be destined for the sea. Aldrnari wondered if their life would be better suited on water than land.

"I should check on the others," Varn said and put his hands on his hips. "Katell used a lot of energy to create her spell. Roparzh may not understand her power."

Aldrnari chuckled. "Someone who has tended to her most of her life should know how to help. I'm sure those two will be fine. But if you need to rest, it's no bother for me. I can navigate and steer on my own."

"I get what you're saying." Varn tapped the side of his nose. "It's hard for me to give up being the captain. I'll leave it to your command. There's more of this ship I'd like to see."

In Varn's haste to leave, Aldrnari almost missed Mavelley waving at him to get his attention. She flew down with a worried look as a row of waves caused the boat to rock.

"What do you see, my love?" he asked her.

"There's a storm ahead of us. I haven't seen one like it before." She squinted toward the distant horizon. "It's like the energy around it is being pulled to the center. We should steer around it as soon as possible."

A flash of lightning streaked upwards from the area she watched. The dull rumble of thunder let Aldrnari know its proximity—closer than he expected and moving fast.

"I'll take a southern route," Aldrnari said as he turned the wheel. "We might hit frozen seas if it stretches too far in the northern waters."

Their ship cut sharply into the waves, becoming more intense from the effects of the oncoming storm.

Then, it stopped.

Aldrnari felt weightless as his vessel lifted from the water. It turned back towards the darkening clouds and landed with a thud onto a large object.

Another massive force knocked into the ship's hull, sending Mavelley tumbling on the deck.

"Hold steady! "Aldrnari shouted.

Panic overtook his ability to do so while the rest of the crew rushed up from below. Aldrnari's concern turned to fear when he realized what was happening. The ship had been caught in the grip of a monstrous creature—one summoned by Crowell.

"Please, take the helm," Aldrnari commanded Varn, who stared over the rails.

Varn shook from his stupor and took Aldrnari's place while the young poet raced to check on Mavelley. She took his hand for assistance. Her wings flexed as she stood and straightened her back.

"I see a ship," she said, looking off the stern. "It's gaining on us."

"Can any of you use magic to break us free?" Roparzh asked and looked at Katell, who clung to him for support. "We can't outrun it like this."

"It's him," Varn said through clenched teeth. "Even if we defeat his summoned beast, we're in no shape to escape the Stormeye."

"I am done running," Aldrnari said and twisted the gem on his bracer. "Countless times I've watched ships reduced to rubble from his creatures. This ship hasn't cracked. And we held back the forces of darkness he so eagerly wanted for himself." He removed one of the throwing daggers from its sheath. "Let's clear the seas from his tyranny."

Aldrnari flung the knife at a limb of the creature as it emerged from the waves. It pierced into the skin, leaving a trail of blood in its wake.

The ship jolted and eased back onto the sea.

Varn regained control of the wheel and turned them south. "You might have—"

His words were drowned out by a roar from the deep and long tendrils bursting out of the waves. The stringy arms reached around the mast, stripping it of sails.

"Move back!" Aldrnari shouted and pulled Mavelley out of the way. "I've seen this massive hydrozoa before. Don't touch it."

"We can handle this," Mavelley said and rushed over to Katell. "Help me blast this abomination back to the abyss."

Katell gave a weary nod.

The two casters began chanting spells as a familiar sound echoed from behind them. Crowell's ship was within range to fire their hooks. Its cannons aimed true to their target, and the snares wrapped around the sturdy rails of The Salty Eleanor.

Aldrnari freed another dagger to hack through the tangle of ropes. Varn left his position at the wheel to help. With the creature gripping their ship, they were unable to pilot away.

"How many are on his crew?" Roparzh asked, prying off some hooks while more shot over their heads.

"At least a dozen, probably more," Aldrnari said and switched to cutting with his other hand.

His knives were meant for piercing and not sawing. He could already feel the blisters forming.

"I've fought with worse odds." Roparzh nudged Aldrnari and pointed out the new set of ropes pulling their ships together. "Save your strength for combat."

Varn let out a deep breath and cracked his neck. "He's right. The true warrior plans how to defeat their enemy before swords are drawn."

A loud groan from below the water let them know Katell and Mavelley were successful with their spell against the creature. Its tendrils curled like it had been placed over a fire. Each one dried and cracked into dust.

Aldrnari turned his gaze to the approaching ship. The Stormeye's leathery sails filled with unholy strength. Shouts from its crew and an ominous voice thundered across the waves—Crowell was summoning another monster.

They were close enough to see his large frame silhouetted by the bright sky behind him.

"Here they come," Varn said as the ships collided.

Aldrnari's stomach tightened, and his heart raced.

The Stormeye struggled to ram their vessel again. It managed to jar them off course, but The Salty Eleanor did not break—much to the surprise of their enemy.

Crowell's crew dropped long boards across the distance of the two vessels. Some managed to swing across while others jumped.

Varn met them with the fury of an immortal and disarmed many in one hit. Roparzh kept pace with him amid blocking enemy swords and chopping off the bindings between their ships.

Aldrnari managed to wound a few with his throwing daggers before Varn kicked them overboard.

Lightning struck the waters ahead, illuminating the form of a giant shark nearing the ship. It slammed into the side. Katell and Mavelley took no hesitation in using their magic against it.

"You should have stayed on the Stormeye," Crowell's voice sounded like it was right behind Aldrnari, but he turned to find no trace of his former captain.

25

"Where is he?" Aldrnari wondered aloud.

Crowell's dark form no longer remained on either ship. Aldrnari thought one of the others defeated him, until his voice returned.

"My power is undefeated." Crowell leaped from the mast toward Katell and Mavelley.

"No!" Aldrnari sprinted toward them.

His feet seemed like they were in mud compared to Crowell's speed. He wasn't going to make it.

Roparzh stepped in front of them as Crowell plunged his sword forward. The blade stuck into the elf who rolled with it from Crowell's momentum. Blood streaked across the deck behind him.

Before the unarmed pirate could recover his weapon, Aldrnari launched his weight into Crowell's stomach. The force knocked them both down.

A pain in his shoulder intensified as Crowell's massive hands lifted him off the ground.

"You found a way to stop my beasts." Each word Crowell spoke dripped with hate. "I should have known you would betray me—and with my brother." He lifted Aldrnari higher and threw him across the deck.

The hardened wood of the mast struck Aldrnari's back, shoving out the air in his lungs. Aldrnari struggled to stand as he searched for help. The women fought for their lives against the swarm of pirates and the summoned creature. Varn had his back to him in combat against a tall figure who moved faster than the others.

Crowell let out a mocking laugh and picked up a fallen saber.

Aldrnari took a step forward but couldn't bear the pain. His knees buckled, and he collapsed onto the ground.

A shriek escaped Crowell's lips.

He gagged from the rope twisted around his neck. Mavelley held the other end while Katell dazzled the pirates around her with flashes of light.

"You gave no mercy on your ship," Aldrnari said and grabbed his throbbing ribs as he stood. "But this is my ship. I've chosen a different path." He took out the last dagger from his bracers. "I know your routes and how to defeat you."

Crowell spat at him in response.

"I know you must have been a seeker of the light," Aldrnari continued. "Give up this destructive life. Return to—"

"He will never change," the pirate fighting with Varn yelled out and took the immortal's blade.

In one swift movement, she let it loose into the air. It spun twice and hit dead-center into Crowell's chest.

"How is this possible?" he gasped. "I cannot die. Not from you."

The dreaded captain staggered as a red stain spilled down from the wound. He sunk to his knees, trying to speak but coughed out blood. Mavelley let the rope free, and Crowell fell face-down onto the deck.

"Your actions led you to this," the pirate who disarmed Varn said and let him restrain her wrists. "I told you to let the boy go."

She lifted her head and looked at Aldrnari with kindness.

"Brittany?" Aldrnari held out a hand to stop Varn from binding her. "Why did you kill him?"

The woman sighed and stared at her fallen captain. "The creatures kept changing him. Each time, he lost more of himself. Once you were gone, there was nothing left of Crowell."

A dull rumble of thunder disrupted Aldrnari's thoughts. They were still headed for the storm.

"Please let me gather the wounded," Brittany said. "We will dismantle the Stormeye at the next port."

Aldrnari nodded while his stomach churned. The carnage of battle left few survivors. Varn recovered his blade from Crowell's body and kept a close watch on the pirates who shambled back to the Stormeye.

"Someone, help me," Katell called out weakly from the other end of their ship. "I don't have the strength to heal him."

She had managed to move Roparzh against the rail. He sat and took heavy breaths, trying to slow the bleeding from Crowell's sword.

"The wound is too deep," he said and winced from pain.

Mavelley knelt beside Katell. "Are you able to save him if I give you some of my energy?"

"I fear it would prolong the suffering if we tried anything." Katell placed a hand on Roparzh. "There has to be something we can do."

"You've already saved me," he whispered. "In the darkness, your voice echoed in my mind. I had to return to you—to the light. My fate would have been eternally lost if you didn't help me find the way back. And I know we will meet again on the other side. Somewhere beyond all the realms is a place where death cannot enter. I sense it getting closer." He gasped for breath to continue. "Please, do not mourn my passing. My peace is coming. Seek out those lost in darkness and bring them back to the light." His hands squeezed hers. "Thank you for saving me, my queen . . . my sister."

His breath stilled, and his eyes drifted up. Katell gently closed them with tears streaming from her own. The boat rocked from the other ship releasing its hold as Roparzh's soul departed.

"His life will never be forgotten," Mavelley said and helped Katell up. "Because of what you did to save him from the darkness, many will find the light. We should prepare ourselves for what is to come. I have a strange feeling about the approaching storm."

Katell looked back toward the elven isle. "Our people will sing songs of his deeds. But my destiny follows your sails."

"We need to do something about them," Varn said and pointed up to the empty mast. "I can conjure a sturdy enough fabric, but I'll need someone to create a force of wind away from the tempest."

The waves pushed from the other side, dragging them closer to the dark clouds. Aldrnari rushed back to grab the wheel, but the ship didn't turn.

"I'm not sure I can steer anymore," Aldrnari called out.

The electricity in the air reflected on his teeth as he gritted them. He wondered if they should have taken their chances on the Stormeye for escape.

He remembered the force of its attack against The Salty Eleanor. His ship remained firm without breaking. The missing sail was the extent of the damage.

"Everyone, get below deck and brace yourselves." Aldrnari managed to point their bow into the brewing torrent of clouds and thunder. "This ship is going to carry us through the storm. I'll lock it down once we're all secured. Hurry!"

Varn lifted Roparzh's body from the deck, and Mavelley led them down the stairs. The storm flashed in anger at Aldrnari, who dared to challenge it. Blinding streaks of lightning made him stumble across the deck to reach the opening.

Against the wind and rain, he pulled with the last of his might to lock the hatch from below.

"We're safe," Mavelley said and placed her hand on his arm. "If this ship held back monsters from other realms, I believe it can withstand anything."

Aldrnari embraced her in a warm hug. Their bodies floated as they kissed. It was as if the fae's magic lifted them from the ground, but something else made them weightless. A fierce wind howled overhead—beyond the boards.

The couple continued to hold each other after the dizzying storm subsided, and they returned to the ground. No waves tipped the boat as an eerie stillness filled the stairwell.

"I should check if it's safe," Aldrnari said and peeked through the cracks of the doorway.

It was hard to see until he pushed it open and stepped out. Above him, a brilliant display of stars filled every part of the sky. One bright streak from a falling star rose from behind the remnants of clouds.

Aldrnari peered at it closer. It was not falling but rising into the heavens.

"Have you ever seen a shooting star go up?" he asked as the others joined him on the deck.

"It looks too close to me." Mavelley shrugged. "Maybe it's part of the spell from the elven isle."

"I thought you were commenting about it being night already," Varn said. "The sun was up when we passed through the storm."

Aldrnari looked across the open sea. In the distance, a tiny pulse of light alerted him of the shoreline. The dim glow reflected off the water further from where the moon hovered in the sky.

"We must be close to Virfell." He rubbed his eyes and stared at the small beacon. "I can see a lighthouse. Can you conjure us some new sails?"

"Aye, lad." Varn smiled and chanted while forming the patterns with his hands.

"I feel a breeze at our backs," Katell said. "I guess this means we're on the right path."

Mavelley's wings lit up while she floated to the crow's nest. "The light will always guide us to the right path."

The newly formed sails caught the wind, leading them toward Aldrnari's homeland. Carried by the sway of the sea, a sense of joy filled him. He had to admit there was always a lingering magic he felt in the waves. They sustained a fire in his soul. And no matter where they traveled, he would keep Mavelley by his side and follow the light.

EPILOGUE

Through the gleam of the signal, the lone keeper stared into the sky with her hands cupped around her eyes. A streak blazed up into the night, causing the girl to rush back down the stairs.

"This is Lighthouse Hope, Lighthouse Hope," she repeated into the crude microphone. "Is there anyone out there?"

Static followed her request, and she leaned back to check the gauges. The receiver lasted countless years, gathering dust until its recent use. A trickle of power was all it needed to run. With the upgrades to the beacon, most of the energy from her family's solar panels diverted to keep it lit.

"Jamie, are you still holed up in that old wreck?" a gruff voice crackled through the speakers.

"The signal is breaking. Can you tell me who this is?"

Jamie tapped the top of her device. Its wires liked to cause issues. Banging on the box fixed most of them.

"You know I don't like to give my name over these things," the voice said and chuckled. "Are you in need of help? Why did you call out on this line?"

Jamie twisted closer to a small window near her chair. Her forehead was nearly on the pane as she looked into the clear night sky. The trail of light from before continued to rise.

"I just saw it," she said, flipping the talk button. "I remember you saying something about knowing one of the designers."

"Yeah, my cousin was working on the coms." A sigh came through the speakers. "One of the storms got too close to the worksite. They saved the ship, not him."

"I'm sorry." She squinted across the sea to a subtle glow along the waves. "I think there might be a storm close to me."

"You're joking, right? They've never shown up near the lighthouse."

Jamie repositioned the rickety telescope on her desk to get a better view. Strange clouds billowed toward the water, not moving with the wind. Lightning appeared to be striking below the surface.

"It's one of the bad ones," she whispered.

Dread crept up on her. Her family never returned from one of their supply runs. She had decided to stay and tend to the lighthouse. Reports over the receiver informed her of a storm that hit before anyone had time to react.

"We should meet," the man's voice cracked again. "There are more survivors on other channels. I've been trying to seek them out. One group found a safe zone. They didn't give me the coordinates yet, but we can plan—"

"Wait," Jamie said, cutting him off. "I see something else coming toward the shore."

"Run!" The receiver lit up from the man's volume. "I've seen the drone videos. Get out of there."

Jamie unplugged the device and hurried to the upper floor. The lamp of her beacon would need to be turned off manually.

She reached out for the switch when an odd sensation stopped her. There was something peculiar about the object in her telescope. It looked nothing like other beings who emerged from the dark storms.

Her older brother teased her that they were portals to an evil world, ready to snatch her into them.

"Could it be?" she asked herself while she raced back down to her office.

She plugged the radio back into the wall.

"Jamie?" the gruff voice sounded worried. "Can you hear me? What's happening?"

"I'm here," she said and held down the talk button to gather her thoughts. "Is it possible—I mean—if bad things come through the storms, couldn't there also be good things?"

"Nothing good follows those storms."

"I have a theory." She steadied the telescope. "It's a ship. There's a large sail, and it looks like an antique."

"Jamie, please . . . be careful."

The line went silent as she focused the lenses on the vessel. Its hull cut through the waves without resistance. The beacon from her lighthouse illuminated the intricately woven sails. Its fabric appeared to be pulling the ship by an unseen force.

Jamie blinked to make sure it wasn't an illusion. Hovering near the crow's nest was a feminine form. A soft reflection from the light made a set of wings visible. The crew of the approaching ship contained something other than the creatures who came through the storms before—something extraordinary was about to reach the shore.

Acknowledgments

I'm eternally grateful to my Creator, who saved me from the darkness. I pray these words are a testament to the Light, showing the mark of the great Author.

This story would not be if not for my wife, Lisa. We met at a Renaissance Faire—I as a poet and her as a fae. The rest became a novel in the making. She is also a fantastic editor!

Crystal, Megan, and Joe: you three have been my staple beta readers. I can't thank you enough for your insight and encouragement through this series.

Thank you to my friends and family, who keep picking up the first editions of my novels and continue to enjoy them.

And last, but certainly not the least, an overwhelming thank you to all who read this book. If I could hug each one of you for spending time in my stories, I would!

From the bottom of my caffeine-ridden heart,
Thank you!

If you've enjoyed this story, please consider leaving a review and find all of Matthew's books on Amazon.

SHADOWS OF ELEANOR

HOLLOWS OF THE NOX

A young scholar discovers a book of ancient sorcery. It challenges his understanding of magic and beacons him to embark upon a journey to find the source of its power.

AWAKENING THE STRICKEN

At the fringes of the elven kingdom, a young sorceress works on perfecting her mother's spells. Yet an evil force may be stronger than her desire to court one of the guards.

THE SALTY ELEANOR

An alchemist born to a blacksmith finds his passion in the earth's elements. Everything changes when he meets someone more enchanting than his weapons.

PASSAGE OF THE FAE

Escaping from his pirate captors, a young poet travels to a place rumored to have fae. But falling in love with one could disrupt their realms—if the worlds weren't already shattering.

THE PYCROFT UNIVERSE

THE PYCROFT PARTICLE

Doctor Patricia Pycroft is set to revolutionize the travel industry with the discovery of teleportation. When strange occurrences happen, her work and faith are questioned.

PYCROFT CONTINUUM

A collection of short stories of those who abandoned the Earth to create a new civilization, ignoring the chaos within.

MUSINGS OF THE NORTHERN POET:

POEMS OF LOVE AND FAITH

ABOUT THE AUTHOR

Matthew E. Nordin is a speculative fiction writer and a Midwestern traveler. He is secretly formulating a series of fantasy novels with a dash of science fiction tales to spice things up. His love of renaissance faires, conventions, and writing workshops have spurred his passion for setting his thoughts into print.

He met his wife while performing with the newly renamed group: Scenery Changes. Together, they specialize in improv comedy shows & acting workshops; creating artistic works & writing; living a simple life & most of all, having fun!

Join in their adventures at
www.scenerychanges.com

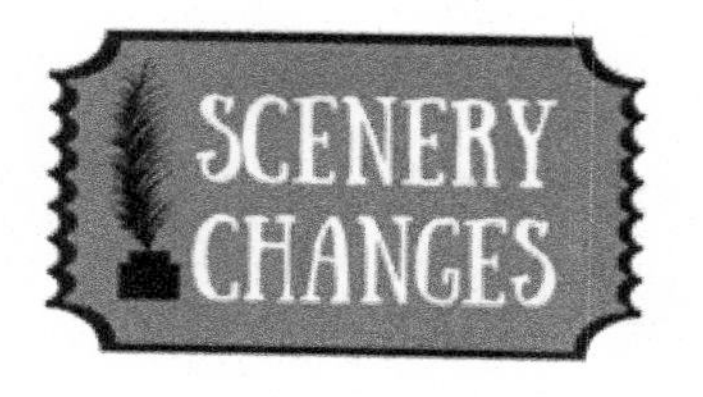

Stage & Scene & In-Between

Made in the USA
Monee, IL
28 July 2022

10315360R00152